PRAISE FOR

SOLIS

"A riveting adventure and a warning . . . a compelling story of a possible future, but one with echoes of past fascist governments. A story of courage and hope but also one of vengeance and loss, raising the question of whether you can defeat the enemy without becoming a monster yourself." **—AllDoneMonkey.com**

"Terrifying . . . yet necessary." **—LatinxInPublishing.com**

"A tight pace and distinct voices bring dynamic energy to this harrowing dystopia, which is perhaps most terrifying in its similarity to our current environmental and political landscape . . . Each character has their own unique traumas, underscoring the very many ways the world is falling apart and the very few possibilities there seem to be for humanity to survive. Readers of Mendoza's *Sanctuary* will recognize some key elements, but no knowledge of the previous book is needed to understand the overwhelming odds these teens—and the world—are facing."

—The Bulletin of the Center for Children's Books

"Set in an alarmingly near future, Mendoza's sequel to her novel *Sanctuary* describes a nightmarish United States in which all immigrants, regardless of current status, are categorized as illegal . . . The plot is tautly written and the pace increases rapidly toward the climax." ***—Booklist***

"Resistance and a fight for freedom in the face of unspeakable horrors . . . the characters are three-dimensional, and their deep connection and care for one another are highlights of the story. A gripping concept . . ." —*Kirkus Reviews*

"*Solis* is an urgently needed antidote to the fear, fascism, and destruction that defines so much of the present world. At the core of this staggeringly beautiful story is a singularly rich, beautiful, and evocative queer love that reminds us that getting to live and dream as our full selves is the ultimate gift. Through Rania and Kenna, Paola and Abby have allowed queer love to breathe and transform—defying narrative and societal constraints, *Solis* finally lets queer readers see themselves fully on the page."
—**Chase Strangio**, ACLU lawyer and transgender rights activist

SOLIS

ALSO BY

PAOLA MENDOZA & ABBY SHER

Sanctuary

SOLIS

PAOLA MENDOZA & ABBY SHER

Nancy Paulsen Books

NANCY PAULSEN BOOKS
An imprint of Penguin Random House LLC
1745 Broadway, New York, New York 10019

First published in the United States of America by Nancy Paulsen Books,
an imprint of Penguin Random House LLC, 2024
First paperback edition published by Nancy Paulsen Books,
an imprint of Penguin Random House LLC, 2025

The Library of Congress has cataloged the hardcover edition as follows:
Names: Mendoza, Paola, author. | Sher, Abby, author.
Title: Solis / Paola Mendoza & Abby Sher.
Description: New York: Nancy Paulsen Books, 2024. | Summary: "Told in four voices, four prisoners, including undocumented seventeen-year-old Rania, rebel against the corrupt and xenophobic government of the New American Republic that exploits undocumented immigrants in deadly labor camps to mine a world-changing chemical"—Provided by publisher.
Identifiers: LCCN 2024024548 (print) | LCCN 2024024549 (ebook) |
ISBN 9780593530825 (ebook) | ISBN 9780593530818 (hardcover)
Subjects: | CYAC: Government, Resistance to—Fiction. | Dystopias—Fiction. | Noncitizens—Fiction. | Mines and mineral resources—Fiction. | LCGFT: Dystopian fiction. | Novels.
Classification: LCC PZ7.1.M47147 (ebook) |
LCC PZ7.1.M47147 So 2024 (print) | DDC [Fic]—dc23
LC record available at https://lccn.loc.gov/2024024548

Printed in the United States of America

ISBN 9780593530832

1st Printing
LSCC

Edited by Stacey Barney
Design by Kathryn Li
Text set in Laurentian Pro

To every child, teenager, and young person who has been forced to pick up the ruins of the world we left you. May this book help light a fire for justice inside of you.

Mateo Ali, you are my fire and my beacon, the reason why I fight.

—PAOLA

×

To Ulla, Mary, and Bird.
You've each taught me so much about perseverance, trust, and the chance to find hope inside each day.

SPF,
ABBY

When tyranny is law, revolution is order.

—PEDRO ALBIZU CAMPOS

JESS

The bus lurches and rocks. Can I even call this thing a bus? There are no seats. Someone must've ripped them out and painted the windows black. My body is dripping with sweat, and there's a thick sour smell like rotten bananas and pee. I can't even swat away the buzzing flies because we are packed in so tight—shoulder to shoulder, chin to eyeball.

We.

It's like I'm one of them now. All of us are chained together by the neck with these spiky collars that were probably meant for dogs. My forehead is pressed into a man's armpit, but I don't say anything. His skin is slimy and probably has a thousand years of dirt and fertilizer all caked into his bristly clumps of pit hair.

Then again, who am I to judge? I haven't seen a mirror since I was thrown into a holding cell almost a year ago, but I know my face must be all shades of nasty. My jaw is too swollen and tender to open fully, my left eye still oozes, and my scalp is a patchwork of scabs and bald spots. Fistfuls of hair, gone, as they grabbed me and yanked my neck back like a Pez dispenser. Groping, pulling, poking.

At least here on the bus nobody slaps me around, trying to break me. A lot of people look past me, or through me. The ones who *do* look at me just glare. It's like they're boring holes into my face, trying to crack me open and see what's inside.

What?! I want to yell. *I'm a skinny white girl from Desert Hills! I'm not supposed to be here!* But I am here. With them. Going who knows where. The only other white person I see is the fat Deportation Force officer who's monitoring us remotely. His angry face is on a screen at the front of the vehicle, and every once in a while he tells people to shut up, cracks his knuckles, or yawns loudly. Sometimes his eyelids droop closed, and I can hear him snoring and farting.

That's also when I can hear everyone around me whispering in different languages. Probably Spanish. Maybe Creole? I don't know. It all sounds like *blah blah blah* to me. Besides, what could they be talking about? There's nothing to do. There's nowhere to go. I can't even tell day from night from whatever we're calling this second. I haven't slept or eaten in I don't know how long, and I'm pretty sure everyone here has pissed themselves at least once.

Sometimes I try to convince myself this is all a dream, but my body hurts too much to believe that. I manage to reach up and touch one of the scabs on the back of my head. Its little bumps and folds of skin remind me of those gross garden snakes that used to slither out onto our front steps back in Desert Hills. When we were little, my older brother, Nick, loved chasing those things, grabbing their slinky bodies with both hands, and shoving them in my face. I'd always yelp every curse word I could think of while Nick jiggled the snakes inches from my nose, forcing me to bat them away. There was one that he squeezed so tight, it looked like its eyes would pop out. I snagged it out of his hands. The snake's skin was hot and slick. I could feel its blood rushing and rumbling just underneath the surface. I remember feeling like I was touching the edges of life and death at the same time.

"Stop!" I yelled at Nick.

"Stop what?" he teased.

After all, *I* was the one squeezing the snake now. I was so scared and mad that I kept clutching the animal tighter and tighter, its eyes bulging, its body going nuts. It took so long for me to get the message from my brain to my hands to just let go! But finally, I dropped the snake and watched it skitter away. I was crying and gasping as Nick watched me.

"You almost killed it!" he snickered.

I can't believe how much I'd looked up to Nick. He was my brother, my best friend, my mentor. I chopped off my ponytail in kindergarten so we could have matching bowl cuts. I named my first teddy bear after him. I even gave a speech at my third-grade assembly that started, "When I grow up, I wanna be just like my big brother, Nicky, and here's why . . ."

Flash forward to the day Nick turned eighteen and immediately marched down to town hall to sign up for our local Border Patrol task force. His goal was to become a Border Patrol officer because our town of Desert Hills, Arizona, was being overrun by illegals. The whole country was. They kept showing up battered and begging—trying to take our jobs, our homes, our money. I had a friend who found a family of illegals lurking in the laundry room of her apartment building. When she reported them to the police, the kids tried to hide in the dryer and the mom flung herself on the ground and had a full-on tantrum. It was pathetic. And Nick was determined to put a stop to it.

I remember after he signed up, he came home tall and thick with pride. Mom started bawling.

"So damn proud of you, Nicky," she rasped. She pulled Nick into one of her chokehold hugs, and his eyes bugged out at me—a little like that slithery snake. "So. Damn. Proud."

Soon after, Nick got selected for a special Border Patrol training down by the US-Mexico border. Every night we hologramed so he could show us the Great American Wall lit up behind him. It was pretty damn impressive too. It stretched the entire length of the border. It was something like fifty feet tall, made of these huge steel slats and mesh on top. There was also barbed wire and electric cables that I heard sent out shocks of ten thousand volts if you got close enough to touch them. The President had spent a boatload to construct it and the Border

Patrol was standing by twenty-four seven so we could finally keep the US safe.

Nick got outfitted with a fancy new AK-87 and immediately formed a crew of friends with matching Border Patrol jackets and ammo. I could feel how bright his smile was even through the screen. I was itching with jealousy. I wanted to be part of the action too, but I wasn't eighteen yet, so I knew they wouldn't take me. It felt so unfair, especially because all those immigrants had their kids working as soon as they could crawl!

Anyway, Nick told us he was psyched to be on the front lines and he'd already helped bagged thirty fresh captures in his first week. He was hoping to get fifty by the end of the month so he could earn a special badge. He got to visit the huge labor camp being built in the Sonoran desert. This is where illegals could go and pay their debts to society by hauling rocks and dredging for new water sources. Nick loved it. He said the Border Patrol wasn't just saving America, it was saving the *world*.

Then, about two months into his training, Nick stopped calling or showing up on our screens. He messaged Mom about being too busy with work to check in, and Mom said of course, but it was clear she was mad. She'd always loved Nick the most. Once again, as Mom said, those dirty immigrants were tearing us apart.

Everything switched into high gear after that. The week before my junior prom, there was some Mexican girl who got blown up at the Wall and the government established a new regiment called the Deportation Force. It was May of 2032, so I was still only sixteen, but the DF started recruiting anyone fifteen and up to help with raids and captures. I was like, *Hell yeah!* I told Mom I was gonna sign up too. She shrugged and said, "Fine."

There was no celebration. No *So damn proud of you* for me. There was just Mom telling me to not overstuff my duffel bag and sending me out to get her more ant traps and cigarettes before I went. And my nine-year-old brother, Gavin, sneering at me while he practiced with his BB gun in the carport. He was pissed at me and Nick for being old enough to go. He was pissed that he was stuck being home with Mom. He was pissed at the world. So instead of saying congrats to me, he spit in the air and then showed me how he could shoot fast enough to break the spit apart.

To be honest, I was excited to join the cause, but I also just needed to get out of Desert Hills and as far away as possible from Gavin and Mom.

I was assigned to do my DF training down at the Wall, which I took as a big honor. I was psyched. Before I headed out with the other local recruits, Mom grabbed me in one of her rare hugs. I thought she might say something vaguely kind or sentimental. Ha. She stank like malt liquor at two in the afternoon.

"Hey," she whispered in my ear. "Keep your legs closed and don't do anything stupid."

I still wonder if she knew what training camp would be like

for me. If she knew how many beefy chests and stubbly beards I'd have to fend off. How many times I'd have to prove my worth at target practice or my stamina with predawn mountain sprints. Whenever I tried holograming with her and Gav, Mom seemed annoyed and impatient. I was pretty sure from the rings around her eyes that she was using again. But, of course, there was no space for me to talk about that or ask her what was up. She stared off beyond the screen or bombarded me with questions about how many times I'd seen Nick or whether I'd caught any illegals with my bare hands, which I hadn't yet.

Ironically, the one time I *did* see Nick was when I got my assignment in the desert, patrolling for migrant caravans and break-in points along the Wall. He was one of the "big brothers" who were supposed to show us how to set up our tents. Which is a laugh because he actually *is* my big brother and he didn't show me shit. The desert shifts were brutal—seventy-two hours with barely enough water to drink. There were tons of beetles and scorpions, crazy windstorms that knocked over my tent, and these shrieky birds that kept nose-diving at me. I felt delirious from heat and exhaustion. I literally had to walk along the Wall and look into any compromised links. Apparently, those coyotes smuggling in illegals now knew how to hack into and deactivate parts of the Wall. There were also reports of illegals ramming the Wall with cars and threatening DF officers with all kinds of weapons.

I saw none of this, though. It was boring and hot and I got bit by some bug that made me break out all over. When I got back from that first shift, I was counting on a hot shower and a good night's sleep. I thought maybe I'd get to regroup at our training hub, process some detention orders. But things were about to get a thousand times worse.

At that point, there were mobs of immigrants swarming the Wall—a new hurricane or something was washing up orphaned kids doing the doggy paddle all the way from Guatemala. Meanwhile, California had announced it was going to secede and be some sort of sanctuary nation-state, which was probably liberal-speak for a socialist commune.

My feeling was—fine. California clearly didn't believe in protecting America, and I heard the only thing they did there was grow and smoke pot. The President soon declared that America minus California would hereafter be known as the New American Republic. We would be getting a new anthem and a new flag, which was exciting. And a new wall sealing off California too. It felt like we were making progress. We were unifying under the New American Republic's vision of what a superpower could be, and I was thrilled by the idea of helping build the new wall around California. I was actually pretty good with a drill and knew how to pour cement.

But instead, my training captain asked if I'd turn around and go right back into the desert for another seventy-two hours. There were images of illegals trying to tunnel their way to El Paso or dive into whatever was left of the Rio Grande. Which sounded like a whole new level of pathetic.

So I wound up being in the desert for a week straight with

nothing but a couple of cans of adrenaline drink and some beef jerky and bubble gum. I barely slept. I was so itchy all over. I had sand inside my ears, my nose, my eyes. It was definitely the worst week of my life. I still can't think about it without panting and grinding my teeth together, wondering why, how, what.

This is what I remember of that week: I was on maybe day three of being all by myself in the Sonoran. I mean, there were other DF within a ten-mile radius, but the only directions I got were "Be on guard!" and "Call for backup only in emergency situations."

I had no idea what an emergency could look like. Was I supposed to dig for illegals like buried treasure or stare through my zoom lens twenty-four seven? I'm pretty sure I was put there solo because it wasn't a heavily trafficked area and the drone reports said it was more important to have DF presence by the water crossings.

The drones clearly didn't pick up on Walter Winnecut, though.

I doubt that was his real name—it's just what came up when I scanned his identification chip. Those were the little lumps in everyone's wrist that showed your ID number, your birthplace, blood type, medical history, et cetera, et cetera. The chips told us who was actually a US citizen and who was illegal. That is, until the illegals started buying fake chips and trying to screw with the system.

"Walter's" chip also said that he was twenty-three years old, which I highly doubted, considering the white hairs poking out of his eyebrows and the wrinkles lining his weathered face. I took a long look at him with my flashlight once he stopped breathing. He had a piece of turquoise hanging from a string around his neck and a phone number scribbled on a piece of paper in his jeans pocket. Also a tattoo on his right shoulder that said *ANGELICA* in fancy script. I don't know if that was his wife or daughter or what. I don't know who he was, really. I just know it was pitch black in the middle of the night and I heard a rustling sound outside my tent.

Mistake number one—I shouldn't have been closing my eyes in the tent, but I was going on four days without any relief and I couldn't stand up straight.

None of this is an excuse, I know.

Mistake number two—I heard a noise, and then I saw the outline of someone creeping around my tent. I don't know if he was scrounging for food or looking for a place to lie down. All I thought was: *Shoot or be shot.*

Except this guy didn't have a gun. He didn't have anything on him. Unless you count an empty canteen and that phone number in his pocket as weapons. He was just in the wrong country at the wrong time. I shot him five times through my tent flap. Then five more out in the open as he lay there on the ground, because I couldn't believe he was dead.

I couldn't believe I'd just killed a man.

I called for backup, but nobody physically came to check in on me or congratulate me on a job well done. The old man got scooped up by a DF drone and carried south. I don't know what they had planned for his body. I just sat there, nauseous and disoriented for hours, and then days. I tried to kick up more dirt to cover Walter's blood stains, but the wind kept swirling everything around, so they reappeared again and again.

I had finally gotten the message that there were reinforcements coming and I could go back to the training hub, when this wretched-looking threesome started coming toward me. They were a mess. The girl was driving a motorcycle—a *DF* motorcycle. She had brown skin and long dark hair. Behind her, there was a little boy clinging to her waist for dear life. There was an Asian guy too, all three of them squeezed onto one seat. I couldn't figure out what the hell was going on—they definitely were *not* DF, that much was clear.

I tried to do my job, I really did. When this ragtag crew came zooming up on the motorcycle, I made them stop. I held my ground. Then I took out my ID scanner and got to work. The little boy stuck out his wrist and scanned fine. But the girl and the guy . . .

It was disgusting. They had these blood-soaked rags tied around their wrists and streaks of red, green, and yellow climbing up inside their skin. I thought I was going to hurl just looking at them.

I'd heard illegals were cutting out their fake chips. Ever since the government ID upgrade, more and more of them were doing it so their wrists wouldn't glow an icy blue. As if their oozing, scabby skin wouldn't give them away instead. I mean, I could've tied them up right then and there and dragged them back to headquarters. I could've made them get into my tent and wait until the reinforcements showed up. But instead, I just stood there—lost.

I kept thinking about Walter's blood seeping into the ground all around us. Was he related to them? Were they searching for the man I'd murdered?

"Name?" I managed to say.

"Um . . ." The girl's eyes were wild with panic. She didn't even try to make something up. "Valentina González Ramirez."

Again—I could've . . . should've done something. Tased them at least.

But instead, I kept going through the intake questions.

"Birth date?"

"July 22, 2016."

I swear, something in me just flipped when she said that. I've thought about this moment so many times since then and how my brain sort of disconnected from the rest of my body. My birthday is July 23, 2016, which is the stupidest reason in the world to stop doing my job. But when she uttered that date, I had this vision of my fifth birthday party when I'd choked on a chicken bone and Nick stuck his finger down my throat. I remembered that day so clearly. I could almost taste the bits of fried chicken and feel Nick's cool skin as he held me up and revived me. Sometimes he was such a brutal asshole, but he'd also been my hero for most of my childhood.

And here I was, in front of this girl one day older than me, who seemed like she was barely upright. All three of them looked like they'd been starved and beaten and who knows what else. I couldn't make eye contact with any of them. I think because I was flip-flopping between shame and disbelief. Somehow I was deciding whether these three people lived or died.

It was too much. I couldn't pull the trigger or tie them up. I couldn't be responsible for someone else dying because of me.

I just stood there for the longest time. We all did.

And then I heard myself saying,

Go.

It felt like somebody else's voice coming out of my mouth and everything around me was spinning and turning inside out.

Of course, the three of them took off before I could change my mind or come to my senses. And then I think there was about five minutes where I just looked around like, *Did that really happen? What did I do???*

I couldn't decide whether I should run after them or pretend everything was normal. But the DF drones decided for me. They'd watched the whole thing play out, and the next thing I knew, there were sirens and I was being handcuffed and muzzled and transported to some horrific cell. And that's when the DF started torturing and interrogating me day after day, week after week. I have no idea how long I was in that little dungeon. I remember different beatings. I remember passing out from the pain. I remember thinking I heard my brother Nick's voice at some point, begging him to get me out of there, telling him I was so sorry and promising I'd be a good girl.

Then there was the trial. It was worse than some of those mock courts we used to have to do in school. I was told to plead my case before a DF jury, and when I opened my mouth to speak, they flashed up some holographic slide show of those three illegals in the Colorado River. They listed out all the taxes and jobs and lives lost because of illegals flooding our borders every day. They lectured me on the ramifications of treason and all the barbaric ways they *could* treat me. And then they threw me into a different holding cell for weeks that turned into months, until someone had the bright idea to have me "work for my redemption." That's when they dragged me out into the screaming sunlight and pushed me onto this hollowed-out bus.

If we can even call it a bus.

There's that word again—*we*.

The truth is, I might as well be an illegal now. As soon as I let those three go in the desert, I became the worst kind of vermin. Now I'm packed into this transport headed to whatever fresh form of hell the DF has devised, and nobody can help me. My ID chip has been reprogrammed so my wrist glows with a steady pinprick of blue light. Just a little reminder: *You are worthless. You will serve us until you die.*

When the bus finally stops, I crash into that armpit next to me and feel the dog collar around my neck rub open my skin. But there's no time to even yelp. A door opens and there are

DF officers in gray fatigues and full-faced tactical masks yanking us out, ordering us to circle up around a flagpole. The red-and-white New American Republic flag with forty-nine stars is lit with its own brilliant light. I don't know whether to salute the flag or cower in front of it. It's enormous, even if there's no wind to make it billow out in all its glory.

It feels like I'm stepping into outer space here, or at least onto the surface of some different planet. The ground is completely razed, except for dark tufts of charred brush. The air is thick with some kind of dust that stings my skin, and it smells like burning rubber. Besides that giant flag, everything here is gray. The ground is gray, the sky is gray, the faces and stooped silhouettes of everyone shuffling by are all gray. They're not people anymore. They're shadows. Thousands of them. Filing past me without even looking up.

This must be the labor camp.

Behind the flagpole, there are rows of gray tents as big as football fields, then a massive wall humming with electricity, and a blanket of drones overhead. To my right, I see a gigantic mining pit, ten blocks long at least, with towers of stadium lights glaring down on it. I'm guessing this is where the prisoners have to dig for aqualinium. Aqualinium is a toxic mineral that a bunch of scientists uncovered in the Arizona desert. It's got amazing geothermal powers or something. The New American Republic is doing all kinds of experiments to get aqualinium to make rain. It's a huge task and it's been going on for years. That's actually why the labor camp was started,

I think, to get these illegals excavating for aqualinium so the New American Republic can finally solve global warming.

And when it does, the New American Republic will truly be the most powerful nation on Earth.

"Hurry it up! In formation!"

There are two DF officers barking orders at us, their voices booming across the open meeting area. They have these hideous mechanized animals with them that look like they're half dog, half wolf, with fluorescent green eyes and metallic fangs. I can't tell whether it's them or the drones circling overhead that make the high-pitched buzzing noise. It could also be from the monstrous-looking pulley lifting a metal cage out of the mining pit. Inside the cage are a mound of prisoners. The cage stops at the edge of the pit and opens, the shadow people spilling out. They are covered in a greenish-colored soot, and a few of them swoon and collapse. I watch as the DF slice at the fallen with batons until they stand upright again.

The shadow people hobble toward the flagpole. They loop around us in another large circle, then form another outside of that, and another, like the layers of an onion. Then, through a large speaker at the base of the pole, we hear the first chords of the national anthem for the New American Republic. There are officers shouting the words at the crowd:

From the mountaintops
To the pristine shores
We shall fight for justice

Truth forevermore
Our New American Republic
Mighty forevermore

I remember how thrilled I was when I heard the anthem for the first time. We all were. We sang it at dinner, we sang it in DF training, we sang it lifting our beers up into the wide-open sky, mixing up our words but still feeling their mighty power coursing through our veins. A crew of people from my training pod got the first stanza tattooed on their arms. We were so sure this was the answer to America's problems. We'd been taught in school about replacement theory and reclaiming our nation's dignity. Getting rid of the illegals and establishing our sovereignty was the only hope for a future! At least that's what I believed.

Now the DF shout-sing these words through their masks, their voices echoing through the speakers on poles. The mechanical canines join in the show too, letting out a chorus of growls and barks. When all of their metal teeth chatter in unison, every inch of my skin shivers. Then we hear a loud blare from the speakers, and the circles of shadow people around us start peeling away. They walk in four lines toward the rows of gray tents, leaving just us new prisoners behind.

"Let's go!" shouts a DF officer. His voice sounds like a pan of gravel through his thick mask. He tugs on the chain connecting us, and we all slam forward, knocking into each other and trying to apologize.

"Shut up!" There's another officer shouting at us as he unlocks our chains and starts shoving us in different directions. Women are sent to the right, men to the left. Our line makes it just a few feet before there's a shriek up ahead and we all stop short.

"I said, let's go!" roars an officer. His mechanical canine snarls on command, circling a prisoner who refuses to go any farther.

"No! No, please!" she whimpers. I don't know why she's doing this. It's not as if there are any other options.

As the officer jerks her backward, a little boy tumbles out from under the woman's ratty skirt. He's flushed and sweaty, probably no more than seven years old.

"¡¿Mamá?!" he squeaks.

"Please, sir, he does not know—"

She lunges for her child, and one of the mechanical canines springs into action. It leaps up behind her, snaps its metal teeth around her hair, and flings her onto the ground.

"¡Mamá, mamá!" the boy cries. "¡Mamamamamamamama!"

The boy tries to run, but he's going nowhere because the officers are too strong, holding him in place.

"Miguelito," the mother moans. Her hair is still in the canine's mouth and her scalp is glimmering with blood. "Todo va estar bien, mi rey." She sobs from someplace deep inside. The boy is wailing and carrying on too. They both look like they're possessed.

I don't want to see this. I don't want to hear their cries or smell their desperation, but I can't turn away. The boy is reaching his arms out, grasping for his mom. And she's still writhing on the ground as the mechanical dog tugs on her like a chew toy. Finally, two more DF officers swoop in behind the kid to bind his hands and stick a gag in his mouth.

"Mmmmmmm!" he screams as they heave him over a shoulder and take him to the men's quarters. I just stand there, dumbfounded.

"I said, to the tents!" an officer bellows behind me. He strikes me with his baton; it sizzles like a hot poker across the back of my neck. Then I hear a mechanical canine approaching, its metal teeth clattering, and I'm moving—past the bleeding mother on the ground, past the shiny flagpole, past a heap of what looks like broken glasses and books. I see the rest of the people from the gutted-out bus ahead, and I do my best to catch up to them.

Together, we plod along a winding dirt path like the most disgusting parade. On either side of us are the long gray tents. They smell abominable—a mixture of shit and body odor.

"To the right!"

"To the left!"

"Hurry it up!"

There are a few more DF officers up ahead, directing us into different tents. The officers all look the same—thick, square shoulders, suited up, with masks that hiss as they breathe. As I get closer, the thought occurs to me that one of these guys could easily be Nick. I have no idea where he's been stationed most recently, but I know one of his dreams was to be an officer at the labor camp.

Wouldn't it be sick and hilarious if he was in charge of me here? I wonder if he even knows that I'm in this transport. I wonder if he remembers we once spit toothpaste into the same bathroom sink or that I showed him Mom's hiding spot for Mallomars and whiskey. I feel my chest getting frantic, my breath getting shallow as I search for him now. Each mask could be him. Each set of shoulders could be the ones that gave me a piggyback to the swing set or shook with laughter when I got food poisoning. I never knew whether I'd get loving Nick or spiteful Nick on any given day.

But does it matter? Would he even recognize or acknowledge me now? It's been almost a year since I saw him in the desert. I've been tortured and abused, labeled a "venomous traitor and threat to the New American Republic." I'm sure Nick has lots to say to me about how I betrayed the cause and shamed the family. There's no way he would forgive me. But if we could just talk . . . maybe . . . ?

One of the officers shoves me toward a tent to my right. The thick gray canvas smacks me in the face as I walk in. The smell is a thousand times worse in here. The place is teeming with flies. There are two dozen cages filled with shadow people. They are sleeping, moaning, crying, hugging each other, whispering, all at the same time in each twenty-four-square-foot cage. I know they're twenty-four feet exactly because when I was in DF training, I had to measure one of the design plans. I thought I was so smart, checking that all the blueprints matched each other so every cage in every tent could be uniform.

"Think of how many captures we can fit in each cage," I remember pointing out at a DF meeting—never imagining I would be one of them.

One of the cages opens, and an officer pushes me in. I stumble into the corner of a metal bunk bed and swear under my breath, but nobody looks up. Most of the women are standing in a tight circle, holding each other's hands. There's someone in the middle, humming a low tune. Some of the women echo her in unison.

"Time to break up the witches' coven!" the DF officer orders. His voice shreds whatever quiet they'd just found. "We got a special guest tonight."

He kicks me with his steel-toed boot and chuckles as I grab a cage bar for balance. Then the women in the tent turn to me. Their bodies seem to pivot in slow motion as they look me up and down. I watch them take in my bruised face, my patchy blond ponytail. My white skin. I've never felt the weight of my skin before, its glaring paleness undeniable.

"She's one of our very own DF," announces the officer. He snorts. "Or, she *was*, until she decided she'd rather rot in here with you all."

He soon leaves the cage and locks the door behind him. I hear someone close by suck in her breath. Dozens of eyes bore into me with a mixture of terror and hate.

And I know they must see only one thing: ENEMY.

RANIA

I am holding Kenna's hand in our cage's nightly prayer circle when the door opens.

"Rania," Kenna whispers urgently, squeezing my palm. "Look at that."

"Time to break up the witches' coven! We got a special guest tonight."

One of the officers has barged into our prison cell, dragging a new victim with him. I hear a communal gasp as everyone takes in this girl's wide blue eyes, her blond hair, and her pale skin.

"She's one of our very own DF," announces the officer with a chuckle. The girl looks around frantically. I have no idea what she's looking *for*. Clearly, there's no escape.

"Or, she *was*, until she decided she'd rather rot in here with you all."

She'd rather be with us? I don't understand. She must have done something horrible, or treasonous. I've never heard of a

DF officer going so far astray that she wound up in the labor camp. I'm honestly curious what crime against the Other 49 she could've committed.

But none of that seems to matter anymore. I can feel from Kenna's tight clasp that there is no sympathy for this shell-shocked traitor. Only rage. And rightly so. Everyone in this cage has a reason to despise this girl and all that she represents. Everyone here has been hunted, beaten, or scarred irrevocably by the DF.

"Wow," says Kenna under her breath.

I'm not sure exactly what she's thinking, but I feel like it must have to do with some kind of revenge. Kenna had watched both of her parents get bound and gagged and thrown into a van by two DF officers. I remember her telling me how they'd looked so manicured and calm. One of them had pale pink nail polish that sparkled as she tied the gag on Kenna's weeping mother and kneed her in the gut.

That had been during the first round of big DF raids back in 2032. Little did we know how much worse it would get.

The DF who brought in this disgraced former officer hovers for a moment, surveying our cage. He seems so pleased to just stand there and see what happens.

Nobody moves, though. Even after the officer locks us in the cage for the night and takes off. Maybe it's a sign that we're too broken already, that they've beaten and tortured all the emotions out of us. We do nothing except stare at this blond-haired, blue-eyed specimen. It's like biology class—which, once upon a time, was my favorite subject in school. Or at least, the one I struggled with the least. I was supposed to get all As in science, then go into molecular biology like my baba.

It's almost laughable thinking about that now. That I would ever be considered some sort of expert on DNA or genetic sequencing when clearly this country wants to wipe out everyone who looks or sounds like me. After being in this camp for over a year, I've lost any thought of becoming a scientist. I can only concentrate on survival. I feel completely hollow and purposeless. Unless I'm with Kenna.

"C'mon," I whisper into her ear. "Let's try to get some sleep."

I know she's bone tired. We're all so malnourished and dehydrated. And Kenna's got the miners' cough. Sometimes it's so bad, I'm scared she's going to break a rib. There's no part of Kenna that looks ready for bed now, though. She swallows hard, blinking back any thoughts of rest as she stays laser-focused on this former DF person crumpled in the corner. Kenna's stare is enough to make me tremble.

"Please?" I murmur, pressing my cheek into her shoulder. I rarely ask her to do anything. Kenna's always been the one with direction or momentum.

"Okay," she replies. "We can let this be. For *now.*"

It feels like she's answering herself as much as she is me, but I'll take it. We lie down on that rusty metal pallet that is our resting spot for the next few hours, and I curl myself into her arms. Even with all the soot, sweat, and fumes that bake into our skin every day, I love the smell of Kenna.

Actually, it's more than her smell. It's the taste, touch, *feel* of her body. It's like she radiates with some inner fire. I don't know how she does it. She's tall and thin, with deep ebony skin and eyes that spark with determination. If anyone's going to make it through this madness, it's definitely Kenna. And she tells me all the time that I'm coming with her.

I still can't believe she sees anything in me. But she does. She nudges my head up and finds my eyes with hers.

"Hey," she says with a soft kiss. "I know you're all about forgiveness and finding what's good, and I'm trying . . . but that girl—"

Then another coughing fit takes over. Kenna gasps and sputters, struggling to get air. I try to hold her, but her whole body is shaking. We sit up for a bit, and I pound on her back to help loosen whatever's caked up in her lungs. That only helps a little, though.

"Here, Kenna." Liliana comes over with a sliver of ginger that she's managed to sneak from the camp's kitchen, where she works. Liliana is like our den mother. She often brings back scraps of bread, bits of potato peels, or even some salt that she hides in her sleeves to get us through the night. Kenna tries to suck on the ginger, but the coughing only gets worse. I continue rubbing her back, and Liliana holds her hand, both of us taking deep breaths *for* her. I don't dare say it out loud, but this cough is definitely getting worse.

It takes forever, but finally, I feel Kenna's breath start to steady and slow down.

"So stupid," she says when she has enough air to speak again.

"Not stupid," Liliana says. "It's cruel what they do to you." She wipes the sweat from Kenna's brow. Kenna loves Liliana—they're from the same town in Vermont, and Kenna was best friends with Liliana's daughter. I feel like they share a bond of unspoken grief and understanding.

And yet, I know Kenna hates having attention like this. She doesn't want to feel weak or impaired in any way. Even though this cough is clearly tearing up her lungs, I think the best thing to do is pretend everything is going to be fine.

I guess I learned the power of pretending from Mama. As Liliana gets up and walks toward the metal cot where she sleeps, I think about how different Liliana is from my mama. First of all, Mama was at least a foot taller than Liliana and all sharp angles. Mama's hands were always busy, but I don't remember her ever squeezing mine or wiping my brow. Mama was scientific and calculated about everything. She probably had an equation worked out in her head to measure how much human contact or affection was most effective. It wasn't that she was cold or withholding. There was just so much going on in her brain that I could never access.

She was brilliant and thoughtful. So was Baba. They were both professors at the Beirut Arab University when I was born. Then Baba got a position doing genetic research at the University of Chicago, so we moved when I was just three years old. Mama loved to tell me how loud I was on that plane trip. How loud I was all the time. Which is odd, because all I remember of those days is our home being so quiet.

Baba was in the genetics lab at least twelve hours a day. Mama and I barely saw him. The few memories I have of those first years in Chicago are of Mama and me picking out books at the library, then coming home to the dim apartment and me eating tabbouleh in my purple bowl. If I behaved well and took my evening bath without a fuss, Mama would sometimes let me light the candles on our little altar to Saint Sharbel while my hair dried. If she was in a *really* good mood, Mama might turn on some music and let me dance on the kitchen floor in my socks. But most of the time, that ended with her saying I was too wild and my stomping was going to knock all the books off our shelves. Which *never* happened!

Those damn books. I always said I wanted to be a scientist or a scholar like my parents. But really, I just wanted to please them and look interested in books since Mama made it seem like being educated was the most noble thing. Honestly, I never liked reading. I hated sitting still, and I wanted all the words on the page to get up and *move* somehow. By the time I got to middle school, it was clear I wasn't as smart as Mama had predicted, and I was done pretending. I wanted to do track or drama club, but she said only if I could get my grades up, so I ran in circles during lunch hour and sang so loud in choir class that I got laryngitis regularly.

Then, when I turned twelve, I chopped off all my hair and got a friend to pierce my nose. When Mama saw it, she got so mad and quiet, she looked like she'd turned to stone. She marched me into the bathroom and pulled out the stud without saying a word. I refused to shed a tear even though it stung like crazy.

I wish I could apologize to Mama for all the heartache I caused her. I know she had so much to handle all by herself—she was diabetic and got intense migraines; she missed her siblings back in Beirut and rarely socialized in Chicago. She was insanely smart and curious but never felt confident enough to put herself out there for a job once we came to the US. And she was trying to raise me to be quiet and levelheaded, but that wasn't me. I wanted to find myself, to be full and alive. I spent so many hours picking at that scab on my nose and staring at it in the mirror. Even when it was red and raw, it made me feel somehow powerful. I felt like I had an inner fire that needed to get out, and it was my job to discover when and how.

But all that changed once the Presidential Proclamation came down.

I remember I was stuck in my room, grounded for another disappointing report card that day. It was just after the President had been elected in 2028 and the "Great American" wall between Mexico and California was erected. But even I knew that walls don't keep people out, ever. Desperate people find a way out of no way, always. Presidential declarations were pretty routine by then. This had to be a big one, though, because I heard Mama gasp even with my music playing.

Baba was at work that evening—of course. We'd been in Chicago nine years by then, feeling safe because of his work visa. But with this announcement, the President formally banned all immigrants from predominantly Muslim countries. It didn't matter if you had a green card, a work visa, or a student visa. If you were Muslim, Christian, Hindu, or an atheist, if you were from Iraq, Afghanistan, Sri Lanka, Iran, or Lebanon. You were no longer welcome in the United States. The President gave people two weeks to leave, and whoever didn't leave became illegal.

Mama called out to me, "Rania, come watch!"

The President looked so giddy as he laid out our fate. I'd never seen Mama as panicked as she was that night. She was messaging all of our closest friends from the university, her cousins who'd come to the US years before us, even her sister back in Lebanon. By the time Baba came home at eleven, Mama had learned that anyone who didn't have a chip would be instantly deported.

Baba didn't even try to dispute these stories or tell Mama to calm down. He just ran his hands through his wisps of thinning hair and gritted his teeth. That's when I knew things were bad and were only going to get worse.

Both of my parents scrambled to figure out what to do. They debated if we should leave. Would Lebanon be safer?

How bad would it get here? Could we have a normal life? Within a few days there were reports of overcrowded detention centers and merciless prisons. After endless conversations they decided we were better off here, even if this country was broken. It cost thousands of dollars, but we got fake chips from a friend of Baba's who sat at our kitchen table and used the same syringe on all three of us. I remember Mama playing music really loudly in case I yelped and me being so proud that I didn't. Also, I remember wondering, *Who is this guy, and why are we trusting him?*

Our fake chips worked—at least somewhat. I mean, I was able to go to school. Baba got fired from the university and had to get a job cleaning toilets in a mall. Mama ordered groceries and rarely went out. At one point, she had to get new insulin patches but refused to order more because she didn't want to type in our home address. Baba got furious when he found out about that. Mama also insisted on locking all the windows and getting us disposable phones that we had to switch out every six months in case we were being tracked. No friends or neighbors ever came over. Our lights were always out by nine P.M. We lived in this sort of secretive, alternate reality for a few *years*. We simply coexisted. We continued. With our breath sometimes making the loudest sound. But at least the three of us slept under the same roof.

It was sometime in the beginning of 2032 when Baba disappeared. I was in high school by then and buried myself in homework every day when I came home, so I didn't even notice the first day or so. Also, I think Mama tried to keep it from me, telling me that Baba had extra work and would be home later than usual. Until one night, I heard her on the phone talking to her sister.

"What's the Deportation Force? . . . Stop that . . . You don't get to cry."

That was Mama. She was too scientific to give in to her emotions. She didn't believe in causing a fuss. She needed to focus, take action, and come up with a viable plan.

The next morning, she told me to pack whatever clothes would fit in my schoolbag and to not speak to anyone as I followed her to the nearest transit station. We got on a bus heading west that had no heat or toilets. We stayed on the bus for two days, and I had no idea where we were going. I kept telling Mama that we needed to go back to our place in Chicago in case Baba came home, but she told me to hush. The only "detail" she shared with me was that we were going to visit an old friend of hers in Missoula, Montana, which I'm pretty sure was a lie.

Then that girl was killed by the land mine between the border of the US and Mexico. Mama tried to keep me from watching the footage on my phone, but I told her I had a right to know what was happening. I could feel her breath coming faster and faster as she peered over my shoulder at the images of the crowds by the Wall.

The next time the bus stopped, Mama grabbed my hand and said, "Come. We're here."

Here was a deserted charging station somewhere near Minnesota. I was starving and had already finished the few snacks I'd packed, but Mama said we had to keep moving, so we started walking for hours on end. When I got too tired to take another step, Mama had us duck into an alley or behind a dumpster for exactly one hour of rest.

The day the DF came for us is still so loud and raw in my head. We'd made it to South Dakota by then and Mama had found us a little diner by some interstate highway so we could finally get a hot meal. I went to wash my face and came back to Mama surrounded by DF officers. One of them yanked her arm and scanned her wrist. When her chip chirped, the officer laughed. He'd just caught his prey.

"Gotcha!" his partner said. "Who else came in here with you?"

"Nobody," Mama answered quietly.

This was the plan. We'd practiced it a bunch of times. We'd sworn that if one of us ever got caught, the other would walk away and not say a word. Mama had tucked a hundred dollars and someone's phone number in my sneaker a few days before. I promised to use it if it was ever needed.

Otherwise, I was to say nothing. Silence would be my superpower.

But as soon as I saw the DF tying Mama's wrists together and pulling her toward the door, I knew I couldn't do it. I couldn't keep our promise.

"Get off her!" I shouted. I was so hungry, but I picked up

my full plate from the diner's counter and hurled it at the officers. Clumps of egg and glistening potato wedges went flying; the plate bounced on a table leg and shattered across the floor. Then the officers were lunging at me, and Mama was screaming, "What are you doing? I told you to walk away!"

And I was screaming over her, "I'm not letting them take you!"

The officers didn't even check my chip. They were too excited to use us as human punching bags. Then they threw us both to the ground and started kicking us in our ribs, our stomachs, our necks. They kicked and kicked until we were breathless and limp, then hauled us onto some van filled with other people they'd hunted. I was vaguely aware of the van moving. We had barely enough room to squat, and we were supposed to sleep and go to the bathroom all in the same place. A few days later, when they dumped us at the gates of this camp, I remember asking Mama, "What's gonna happen to us now?"

I knew she had no idea, but I just always expected her to have some sort of answer. I expected her to silently hold up the world.

What I didn't realize was that Mama was already so sick.

We were brought to a tent with a bunch of cages inside. Each cage had dirt floors and about forty metal sleeping pallets. They were kind of like bunk beds or shelves stacked one on top of another. Mama and I were told to strip down so we could wear these burlap-sack uniforms. I knew she was trying to be discreet, but there was no place to hide. When Mama took off her clothes, I saw purplish-green splotches climbing up her legs and torso. She was rail thin too.

"Did you already run out of insulin?" I asked.

"Shhh," she commanded. Clearly, the answer was yes. Days of fleeing without food, water, or medicine had winnowed her down to skin and bones. She didn't say anything, of course, but she needed help.

"Please," I said to the DF officer taking our clothes away. "Can she see a doctor? Or at least get some juice?"

The officer thought that was hilarious and smacked me with the back side of his hand. Mama wiped my bleeding lip and again said, "Shhh. I'm fine."

She wasn't fine, and we both knew it. Still, it was shocking how fast it all went. These were the beginning days of the camp. The DF had us pouring concrete and carrying giant steel pipes to reinforce the camp's wall. One day, I saw Mama's knees buckling and tried to take some of the piping from her load, but she shooed me away. Soon after, she fainted and got a huge knot on the back of her head that she insisted was nothing.

But that night, she kept whimpering next to me on our cot.

"Mama? Are you okay?"

"Shhh," she answered.

"Mama, please. Can I look at your head?"

"Shhh."

"Or try to get you some water?"

"Shhh."

Her last breaths on Earth were used up telling me to be quiet.

"Shhh, shhh, shhh," she kept repeating, until she made no sound at all and I knew she was gone.

The next morning, my dead mother's skin was cold and hard as I clung to her. Her face was gray and set in a frown. I didn't want to leave her, but if I didn't report to roll call, I knew I'd be punished. So I wrapped her in our one scratchy blanket and left her there, wordlessly.

I did what you told me to do, Mama.

I did not say anything.

I wanted to shriek at the top of my lungs, especially when I came back to the cage that night to find an empty pallet where Mama used to lie. Still, I stayed silent.

I don't know what I did or how I survived after Mama was gone. There were days, weeks, maybe a month that passed where I didn't say a word. I poured concrete. I hauled rocks. I woke up each day surprised and furious that I was still alive.

Then Kenna came.

Actually, first the pterodactyls moved in. That's what I call the giant cranes that started tearing at the earth all around us. The ground just crumbled from the pressure, making an enormous crater. We'd been through so many tornadoes and earthquakes, the years-long drought and blistering heat. I didn't need a fancy science degree like either of my parents to know that the entire planet was shriveling. The aquifers were bone dry, and the new president loved to appear in ominous hologram addresses announcing that he was going to win the water race and find some new source of irrigation.

The cranes dug out an enormous mining pit with lots of slopes, burrows, and tunnels. "That's where you come in!" bellowed one of the DF officers standing on a platform in front of the New American Republic flagpole.

A small army of DF surrounded us with rifles and mechanical canines that snarled and snapped at the air.

The officer in charge explained that we were finally going to be able to repay our debt to this great nation by going into the mine and digging for a new mineral they'd found in the Earth's crust, called aqualinium. The government was sure that if harnessed properly, aqualinium would be able to open up the skies and make rain. No one knew if aqualinium existed anywhere else on Earth, so, at least for right now, Arizona was where the future of water lived.

The world was so parched by this time. All the most dire predictions about climate change back in the early 2020s were like fairy tales compared to what we'd been living through since about 2025. Then there was the nuclear disaster in Ukraine, the crazy wildfires that burnt down half of Canada, and at the start of 2033, scientists predicted that the Philippines would be underwater by the end of the year.

But somehow, aqualinium was going to be our saving grace. The New American Republic was experimenting with how to break it down, isolate it, and then get it into the atmosphere to produce clouds and condensation so they could make it rain on command.

Of course, aqualinium was all kinds of toxic. It smelled like sulfur and was structurally fragile—which is why they needed our bare hands, our fingers, our forced labor to dig through the crumbling earth for these precious pellets. We were each issued a small pickaxe, a hammer, and a headlamp. Then, once we got a chunk of rock free, we were to pull apart the precious pebbles of aqualinium by hand and dump them in a bucket every hour, while our skin blistered and stung.

If aqualinium was the world's savior, it would also be our death.

After the first day in the mine, my fingernails were shredding. My bones felt like they were screaming in pain. I had bits of aqualinium slicing open my palms. Even with the little fans they had and the ventilation tubes down in the tunnels, I couldn't stop coughing. There was a blanket of ashy green soot everywhere, burning my throat.

"I guess we should just be thankful we're still standing, huh?" Kenna said when I met her in line for food. At first, I didn't realize she was talking to me. I rarely talked with anyone unless I was at our cage's nightly prayer circle.

"My name's Kenna," she said. "I came in with the newest transport."

She looked like she was probably around my age, but her soulful eyes were much older. There was something so stunning and fierce about her gaze.

"And you are . . . ?"

"Oh! Um . . . Rania."

I was honestly surprised. I couldn't think of the last time

someone had wanted to know my name, or really anything about me besides my immigration status or my ability to withstand abuse.

"Don't take this the wrong way, but is it 'Umrania' or 'Rania'?" Kenna asked. "I don't want to mess it up."

I had to laugh. Which, again, I hadn't done in I don't know how long. "It's just . . . Rania," I told her. And she gifted me with the most brilliant smile.

I still don't know if I believe in love at first sight, but I felt something ignite when Kenna smiled at me. She was filled with some current of electricity. Or maybe it was defiance. I didn't know how to explain it even to myself—this sudden aching to be near her. I was so surprised by how intimate and honest we could be with each other almost immediately. And when she sang for the children in our cage before bed, everything else seemed to fade away. Kenna's voice came from somewhere so deep and calm, I felt as if I was falling into her song, and I didn't want to ever return.

I'd never thought of myself as queer until I met Kenna, until I started talking to her and hearing about her life and wanting—no, *needing*—to be a part of it. At first I thought I liked Kenna despite the fact that she was a girl, but I soon came to realize I loved Kenna because she was a girl. I couldn't believe how much I loved her in the midst of all this misery and suffering. Kenna awakened something in me that felt so intense and undeniable. It was a longing, a hope, a dream that kept me alive. I guess when you live on the edge of death, there's no reason to hide from yourself. Everything was ending and beginning at the same time.

The sirens go off for morning roll call, and there's an announcement to report to the flagpole for harvest.

"Another harvest!" I whisper to Kenna, shaking her awake.

"What? When?" she asks.

"Now."

She stifles another cough and kisses me. "It's okay," she says. "It's just rainbows going boom."

I have to smile. This is what one of the moms in our cage told her little daughter when we were lining up for the last harvest and the girl was freaking out.

"Rainbows going boom," I repeat, kissing Kenna back and squeezing her tight. I wonder what Mama would say if she could see me holding Kenna in my arms. She would be shocked for sure. She would probably be angry and disappointed too. Or maybe she would be grateful, maybe even happy, that in the middle of this nightmare I found love. I want to believe that she would accept me and admire Kenna. Mama and I arrived here over a year ago, and she was gone within that first week. Then Kenna came exactly nine weeks and five days later. I only know that because Kenna keeps track of every day that we've survived together. She's my keeper of time, making this world bearable somehow.

"Come on," Kenna urges now as she stands. "Harvest."

We used to have harvests maybe once a month, but lately they're more and more frequent.

The harvests—where the DF officers decide who will live and who will die.

The harvests—where they select a dozen of us "randomly" by making our chips flash to signify our fate. Only it's not random at all. It's clear that they're picking the people who look sickly or too weak to work anymore. They're using us as human guinea pigs in this grand attempt to produce their artificial rain.

The harvests—where anyone can be taken, really. We're all so debilitated in one way or another, whether it's from the fumes in the mine, malnutrition, dehydration, or sheer terror.

"Let's go," urges Liliana.

We shuffle out of our sleeping quarters with hands clasped tightly and join the formation by the central flagpole. There are rows of cadaverous-looking people lined up in front of that gaudy red-and-white flag, waiting to hear their fate. Our camp now has about three hundred tents, with maybe two dozen cages in each tent—I don't need to do the math to know how overcrowded we are here. Even out in the open, we're all packed in so close I can smell everyone's stale, frantic breath.

"Attention!"

First, an officer gives us the lecture about how the New American Republic is the greatest nation on Earth and how it is going to save the planet when it is able to produce the much-needed rain. We, the "illegals," have *stolen* from this land and owe it to the New American Republic and the world to work toward this noble cause. While the lecture is going on, there are officers sauntering up and down the lines like proud peacocks. I can't see their faces through their masks, of course, but I imagine them beaming with pride.

And I have to wonder . . . are they actually *looking* at us? Can they see our broken bodies or hear our hearts beating, our blood pumping through our veins?

I think of Mama's favorite proverb: *The three great mysteries: air to a bird, water to a fish, humanity to itself.* She loved to say that to me whenever I had too many questions for her to answer. Now I want to tell her we're destroying the air, the water is gone, and it looks like humanity is next.

As the sun starts to leak out from the horizon, the DF officers order us to sing the New American Republic anthem as loud as possible. They love to time it so that those selected for the harvest feel their chips go off on the last note. I sing the anthem extra loudly today, because I can tell that Kenna's breath is still raggedy as she tries to stifle more coughing and I don't want anyone else noticing. I'm also trying to sing through all the fearful noise in my head, all the quaking in my skin.

It doesn't work, though. The anthem always feels too fast when I know what will come afterward. Even if I hold out the last note until the bitter end, the chips will still start buzzing and flashing that icy blue. Those chosen will be forced to raise their hands above their heads. There will be gasps and pleas for mercy as the DF round up everyone with a flashing chip, herding the victims forward as they cry . . .

No!

Please!

Yah mira bacha he!

Silvouplè non!

I don't understand all the words, but I can guess. And I have to admit, the first thing I do when I realize Kenna and I are both spared today is laugh, cry, and pee myself a little all at once. I can't help it. The release of knowing we're still alive and together for at least today washes over me.

But then we have to watch.

I'm scrambling to see if I recognize any of the chosen faces, but it's already too horrific. Some of the victims are shrieking, grasping at the air between them and whatever family they have left. Some of them are already so close to death, they can only stare at the ground as they hobble toward the periphery of the mine. Maybe saddest of all are the ones who walk with no expressions—stoic and resigned. The DF force the selected prisoners into the harvest cage and lock them in.

Then a pulley lifts the cage up into the air and dangles it over the mine. The canisters are lit. I've never seen a canister up close because they're posted on these metal parapets along the wall of the camp and heavily guarded. But we've been told that the canisters are filled with some sort of mineral compound that includes our precious aqualinium. Somehow, the minerals get shot into the sky and start clustering in midair. Then we wait as these ominous-looking clouds form, swirling and hissing over the cage.

Every harvest is more gruesome than the last—the clouds burst into flames or spit fire on the dangling cage. Sometimes they spew out like volcanic ash. They make a haunting sound and reek of noxious fumes. Often, the people chosen for harvest die right there on the spot, the liquid burning them. It is the most savage thing to see, their bodies blistering and writhing. But there are those who make it through a harvest, and it's maybe even worse. They can barely stand; their bodies are crippled, covered in gruesome sores. Their eyes fog over like they're stuck between this world and the next. The breathing dead, we call them. They are sent to the medical tent, where I've heard they're used for experiments so the DF can study and refine their aqualinium mixtures. When I see those poor souls being carted off to the medical tent, I can only pray for them to die quickly. So they don't suffer.

One, two, three, release!

There's a thin whistling sound as the mineral compounds get vaulted into the air. The ground is spinning, the air is so hot. The smell is putrid, even from this distance. Kenna draws me into her shoulder so I don't have to see whatever happens next. I know Kenna thinks it's always better to witness it all. I can picture her long dark lashes pulling her beautiful face into a concentrated stare. She will watch every moment, every movement. She'll stare so hard that the atoms in front of her will split from the force of her gaze. This is who she is and this is why I love her. And I am thinking all of these things when I hear the air crackling and steaming. The sizzling drops of manufactured rain pelt the cage, and we hear cries of unfathomable pain.

Help! No!

Min handia!

Miluji tě!

I don't understand all the words, but I can guess. Especially when I hear,

Adéu!

LILIANA

Querida Valentina,

I know you can't possibly hear me, but I need to say these words. I whisper them into the night. In Spanish, of course. Isn't that funny? We worked so hard for so long to make English sound natural on our tongues because I was afraid they would come for us. But they came anyway. And now I refuse to be afraid. These words come from the deepest places of my heart, raw and true. Like a prayer. A prayer I have been saying for almost a year since I arrived in this prison, whose sole purpose is to strip me of my humanity.

Mi'ja. Where are you?

I must trust that somewhere, somehow, you and Ernie are safe. Vali, please, be patient with him. I know he can annoy you sometimes with his whining and his talk about fútbol fútbol fútbol. But you must take care of him. I hope you followed the map I gave you. Every night I dream we will be together soon. I believe this. I do. This is what makes me strong and gives me breath even in the darkest moments.

I close my eyes and I paint a picture of your smiling face. I see the sun warming your skin and you and Ernie laughing with Tía Luna.

I try not to ask myself how this all is possible, how the two of you made it from Vermont to her place in California. I'm too scared to imagine what the journey across this country might've been like with the Deportation Force chasing you. My head starts spinning and throbbing, and then all I can see is that last time we were all together at the bus terminal.

Alien apprehended! Alien apprehended! *There were so many DF shouting into their speakers, swarming in from every side.*

I can still feel the officer's knee pressing into my back as he pinned me to the ground. I kept mouthing the word Go! *Begging you to get out of there before it was too late. I hate that you had to experience that. I hate that we can never erase it from our past.*

But, Vali, we must look forward. We must have faith. Yes, this is so hard. And yes, our prayers don't always get answered the way we want them to. Sometimes the waiting is the hardest part, and I cannot change that. It hurts more than the kicks. More than you being ripped away from me. More than the unanswerable questions lurking in the night. The waiting is where all the hurts and doubts and fears get to claw at us and there is no way to push them down. But still, I choose to believe in the goodness of all creatures and in miracles great and small because I think it is the only way we can survive.

Mi'ja, I want to tell you about a miracle I found in this brutal labor camp. Soon after I first came here, I heard a bird singing. Her song was so beautiful, the melody tripping and twirling, and I thought, maybe a sparrow? A mourning dove? How do they find water and food in this ruthless, dry heat? I only heard it singing at night, though. Never during the day. When we stepped outside our tents each morning, I searched the skies. All I saw were insects. One day, I was sure I found a birds' nest by the outhouse, but when I got close, I realized (too late!) that it was filled with some sort of wasps, and they stung me everywhere.

I know, so foolish. But it's okay. As I lay there that night, my skin still screaming, I heard the bird again. This time, it felt so close. Maybe it was trapped inside our cage? So I followed the sound. I tiptoed quietly—there are so many people just in my area alone, it's difficult to move about without stepping on someone. As I followed the beautiful sound through the maze of broken bodies, I became certain that it was inside but at the far end of our cage. When I made it to the other side, I held my breath so I could listen to the song above all the cries and whispers.

And you know what, mi'ja? It wasn't a bird at all! It was Kenna! Your Kenna! I could barely get her name out of my mouth. I was shaking, tears streaming down my face, but finally I was able to say, "Kenna! Kenna, it's me, Liliana!" She turned toward me. A howl burst from inside of her. It was filled with so much hurt, the sound almost crushed me. She ran to me. Our arms locked around one another. Words tumbled out of our mouths in spitfire succession.

"Where is Vali? Ernie?"

"Are your parents okay?"

"When did you get here?"

"Where do they have you working?"

"Are you healthy? Did they hurt you?"

Physically she isn't hurt too badly, but she is not the same lighthearted Kenna you knew. Mi'ja, her parents were taken, as was her entire family. She thinks they are dead because they aren't here with us. Maybe this is the best outcome. I'm so sorry to tell you this horrible news. The torment of losing your entire family is almost more terrible than death. But Kenna was so happy to know you were not here. Her eyes lit up when I told her I sent you to California with Ernesto. We laughed with so much joy at the possibility of your safety. We cried tears of happiness knowing you weren't here with us. Kenna and I slept side by side that night. We held hands, our fingers interlaced until the morning.

Wonderful, beautiful, glorious Kenna gave my heart rest.

Valentina, I'm not going to lie to you. This place they've brought us to is terrifying. They lock us in cages and give us just one hot meal a day. We are packed in so tight, we share each other's nightmares. We pass around fevers, flus, the never-ending miners' cough. There is always so much crying and moaning when the night comes. The cages are terribly hot, and they smell like feces and urine.

The harvests are the worst of all. These are the cruel experiments where the DF try to make it rain. Do you know about this? I wonder. Have you heard about this miracle mineral that the Other 49 has found and is forcing us to dig from the ground? It is called aqualinium, and they are sure that once they know how to harness its power, it will be the perfect tool for weather manipulation.

Vali, I tell you these things not to scare you, but to make sure you know that we can do things that feel unbearable, that each day, we get another chance to fight. Mi'ja, from the moment you were born, I have been so proud to call you my daughter. I still remember Papi handing you to me, so warm and slippery from my womb. You did not cry at first. You were too busy looking around the room, taking in our tear-soaked faces. You pursed your lips and gazed at us for the longest time, your tiny forehead pinching together as if you were asking, Are you all ready for this? *And then you let out the sharpest, most piercing yell. It wasn't a scared or sad sound. It was as if you were calling us all to action. Like you were summoning up all the souls of the past, present, and future, demanding our attention. The partera jolted. Even Papi looked stunned.*

Vali, I knew in that very moment that my life was forever changed—that the world was forever changed too.

Papi used to accuse me of being afraid of you. The way you grabbed for my breast and pulled yourself up to standing in just a few short months. I always laughed and told him he was silly, but I see now that he was a little bit right. Not afraid, so much as in awe. I had never met someone as mighty and determined as you. We had to get you stitched up three different times in that first year because you kept charging at the table or jumping off the rocks in the hillside. I remember abuela asking if everything was okay, and I answered, Ask her! She's in charge!

But, Valentina, I don't want your bravery to be your burden. I don't want you to feel that you, and you alone, must save our family. I never wanted that for you. You know what my biggest regret is in this moment? That I didn't buy you those jeans you wanted with the special design on the pockets. I still don't know why they were so special to you, but it doesn't matter. I could have taken the money from our cashbox and given it to you for your birthday. I wish I had done that. I wish I could give them to you now, or at least a shoulder to cry on or an extra hour to brush your hair. I wish I could lie next to you as you sleep—watching you breathe in and out, your brow smooth and calm, your wild dark hair so beautiful in the night.

I hold my hand to my heart and give thanks that it is still beating. I listen for the birds' song at sunrise, just as I taught you. It's hard to do here. I only hear the raspy cactus wren, who sounds so angry all the time. Often there is no sunrise or sunset, just a sky filled with different shades of murky haze, so we do not know day from night. There are towers with bright, hot lights on all the time. The drones swarm overhead with a constant buzzing. They track our every movement. We cannot escape them.

The first siren is some time before dawn. We must report for roll call within five minutes or there is a public beating. Then we go to the harvest, and if we survive, we get our breakfast of stale bread. Whoever lingers to get the bread is usually late, and then they are disciplined too. Most people line up for the transport into the mine. There is one huge underground mine now, and two more being dug. Everyone in the mine must use the simple tools they give them to dig at the silt and rock, to mine for this precious aqualinium.

The DF are destroying us to find water, to rule this withering planet even if they are the only ones left here to live on it. Maybe that's the point. They can have complete dominion over this shriveling, restless world and everyone else can gasp while the rains drown us out.

I still don't know how I was assigned to work in the kitchen. Of course, I'm eternally grateful for it. Don't get me wrong, the work is grueling and disgusting. There are just five of us to haul in crate after crate of rotting onions or sacks full of rice that are crawling with worms. My first week here, I dropped a pot of boiling water and scalded both of my legs. I was roaring in agony, but the other women in the kitchen stuffed a rag in my mouth and told me to stop or the DF would come to take me away. A woman named Nelini pressed baking soda onto my bubbling skin and repeated over and over, "You do not feel anything." She said it until I believed her. Her voice soothed me even though my skin was blossoming with hot welts. Then she offered me her hand, and when I took it, she pulled me up to standing.

Nelini soon became one of my closest friends here. We scrubbed, boiled, and chopped next to each other every day. She taught me how to use every last crumb or stalk because there is never enough to feed everyone and people plead with us for just one more cup of broth, just another spoonful of beans. Nelini showed me how to survive here and how to help others. Salt became our best tool to try and heal people's wounds from the mine. When the DF officers who oversaw us in the kitchen weren't looking, we put pinches of it into the folded sleeves of our burlap dresses. Once we got back to our cages, we rubbed it on people's wounds to try to kill any bacteria that might be in them. We never have enough of it. There is always more harm and pain than we can fix with our meager salt, but that doesn't stop us from trying.

Nelini was brought to the camp a few months before me. Her first job was working the mine, and her lungs were damaged because of it. I don't know why or how she was moved from the mines to the kitchen, but in the end it didn't matter. Her lungs were filled with the dust particles of aqualinium, and the miners' cough eventually wreaked havoc on her body.

Toward the end, Nelini couldn't go more than a few minutes without being overtaken by her cough. I tried to cover for her in the kitchen. I worked harder and faster than I ever have in my entire life. I did my job plus *Nelini's job, and when the coughing fits were really bad, I hid her in the outhouse. I needed to keep her out of sight and away from the officers' murderous eyes. I knew if they saw how bad her cough was they would send her to the harvest.*

One night, I was trying to figure out where Nelini could hide during the day because the outhouse had become too dangerous. That morning an officer had found two children hiding there during their work shifts. He was so furious, he forced them to submerge themselves in the sewage. They pleaded for another punishment. He pulled out his gun and said, "It's the shithole or a bullet." They didn't have any other choice. They lowered themselves down into the hole as the guard roared in laughter. He let them get out after a few minutes.

Nelini overheard the entire scene play out as she hid in another outhouse. I have never seen her so incensed as she told me what happened. She said next time she would not stay quiet. I knew Nelini well enough to know this was not a threat but a promise. She needed a new hiding place.

I was lost in these thoughts when Nelini came to my bed and grabbed my hands. She pulled me close to her.

"I need you to listen to everything I say, Liliana."

"Of course. I always do."

"Come closer. No one can hear this."

I did as she asked.

"There's a resistance group called SOLIS. They work with California. They're trying to get us out of here. I'm part of SOLIS. You can trust them. Everything you need to know is in the outhouse."

"Wait. What? Nelini, what are you talking about? A group? Who—"

"Shhh. Listen, before I start coughing again. In the north outhouse, the one next to the second tent, the last brick, behind the hole, there are papers that explain everything. You can communicate with them. Tell them I'm dead."

"What? No! Why would I do that?"

"Liliana, you know I'm going to the harvest soon. It's just a matter of time. And you're the only one I truly trust. You're the only one that can help SOLIS get people out. As soon as you can, go to the outhouse and follow the instructions. Promise me you'll do this."

"I . . . I . . . don't know."

"Liliana, you can't just accept what they're doing to us. You have to fight! You have to—"

She didn't say another word that night. She couldn't because the cough overtook her. It was relentless. Her body heaved. Her lungs fought for air. Her eyes seared into me. She did not need to speak to me for me to understand what she was demanding. I had to help SOLIS.

Vali, I felt I could not do this. I was not brave like Nelini. It felt reckless for me to do what she was asking of me. She taught me how to cook in this camp. She taught me how to help people who needed their wounds cleaned or how to get the sick an extra piece of bread.

Nelini did not teach me how to plot an escape or lead an uprising. I did not feel equipped to take Nelini's place. Simply put, I was too scared.

All I could think about that night was how she had kept this secret from me for six months. She lied to me for the entire time. She could have been caught communicating with SOLIS, which would have put my life in danger along with hers because we were always together. The guards never would have believed I knew nothing about her plans. I know it seems ridiculous to be concerned about putting my life in danger when I am already at the edge of death every minute. But I was still mad and hurt. Regardless of how I felt, I stayed by Nelini's side that night because she was my friend and she needed me. She could barely breathe, and all I could do was be there with her.

The next morning at the harvest, Nelini and I were standing next to each other. I took Nelini's hand in mine. Her hand told her life story. It was warm just as she was, strong and sturdy just as she had been since I'd met her. Her fingertips were callused from the hard work she endured here and in her life before. She held my hand so tightly, I felt as if she was telling me everything was going to be fine.

Nelini was desperately trying to stay quiet. Her body convulsed with every cough she held back. I wanted to hug her, to give her some comfort, but drawing any attention to us would have only been bad for the both of us. Instead of hugging her I just stared at her wrist. Our wrists glowed a constant icy-blue light. Before we were brought here, when we lived on the outside, a blue light was a death sentence. A glowing chip made you an easy target for the DF. A glowing chip let the world know you were not meant to be in the US, you were undocumented, you were illegal.

But here, in this backward hell, a glowing chip kept you alive. It was the flashing chips that meant you were sentenced to go to the harvests.

That morning I could not take my eyes off of Nelini's chip. As soon as it started flashing, I cried out as if it were me being sentenced. How could I be losing Nelini after all that I had already lost? How could God be so cruel? I wanted us to disappear or go back in time. I wanted us to be anywhere but here.

Nelini pulled me into her and only whispered one word: "SOLIS."

Then she was ripped away from me by a DF officer. What happened next is a blur. Her arms thrashed about as she tried to claw, tear, and split the officer apart. Her wild strength overpowered the DF officer, and three more had to come to his aid. They each grabbed one of her limbs and lifted her off the ground. As they carried her toward the cage, she screamed from the depths of her soul one word over and over.

"LIBERTY!!! LIBERTY! LIBERTY!"

They threw her into the cage and slammed the door shut. She stood up and looked for me. When our eyes locked, she raised her arm in the air. The blue light flashed from her wrist, and with her fingers she formed the letter L. *The clouds swirled and churned into a greenish monstrosity. Thunder crashed above us, and poisonous rain poured down. I wanted to close my eyes, but I knew Nelini would want me to bear witness to her death. Her screams were louder than the thunder. The poison that fell from the sky pummeled her. She was the last one standing, her arm raised, an* L *in the air, but eventually she collapsed. Her body could not withstand their hateful experiment. I watched them cart away her lifeless body. My heart shattered. Nelini found her freedom in death. But what about us?*

After the harvest, we were ordered back to our stations. I boiled and chopped and searched for some sort of guidance. How was I going to go on without Nelini? What was I supposed to do about SOLIS? Should I follow Nelini's instructions? I was terrified that I would be jeopardizing everything for some foolish idea of salvation. And I needed to stay alive so I could see you and Ernie again!

After dinner, I like to bring together the people of our tent for a sort of prayer circle. We do this every night, before we lay our bodies down. It is astounding how many new people come every day. Some have been living in the Other 49 for years, others have just arrived. When I ask those who recently immigrated why they insisted on coming to this rotten country, they say they didn't know it was so bad, they didn't believe the rumors, home was somehow worse. The Other 49 has managed to keep the facade of normalcy to the rest of the world while we are torn limb from limb in the secrecy of this labor camp. In this sick, twisted world, the Other 49 needs a steady stream of prisoners to keep coming because they must keep the mine going; those that die must be replaced.

I guess I'm the leader of this nightly ritual, but mostly that means that I say the first prayer aloud and then ask who wants to say the names of the people they have lost or from whom they have been separated. There are so many names, Vali. The list is never-ending. The names of the dead. The names of the sick. The names of those who have disappeared but are never forgotten. Every night, there are more and more names to add to our list of souls who've passed on, and there are fewer and fewer people coming to gather and pray. I don't know if it's because they are sick, or tired, or have lost their faith. I don't bother the people lying down. I don't ask any questions. I just listen to those names and have faith that saying them aloud can bring them closer in some way.

I recite your name and Ernesto's, of course. Saying your names brings a kind of calm to me. I picture you as a little girl, reaching up to the kitchen table and grabbing a fistful of mangos, or swaying your hips and clapping in the hallway while I play a vallenato, your long braids swinging. I think of Ernie's toothy grin and the way he can never sit still. Some days, saying your names is the only thing that brings me peace.

But tonight is different. There is no moment of peace, no sliver of calm. I say your name. I say Ernesto's. I say Nelini's. And then I surprise myself by asking, "But these prayers . . . are they enough?"

VALI

"Drop!"

I've heard that word so many times now my body responds without even thinking about it. Within a second, I'm in the straight-arm rest position, though there is nothing restful about it.

"Push 'em out, soldiers."

"One!" Twenty-four men and women shout in unison as we do a push-up.

"Two!" Quick, determined, and strong voices bellow out into the desert air.

We are all here for one reason and one reason only: SOLIS's Special Ops team known as Condor.

I don't count when I'm doing push-ups, sit-ups, burpees, or any other exercise they make us do. I stopped counting after the first day of boot camp. I didn't feel determined or strong when I counted, both of which I needed to be in order to graduate from this inferno. Instead, I mouth the numbers, but in my mind, I repeat my prayer, my mantra, my reasons for being here:

Mami, Kenna, Rosa, Tomás, Volcanoman, Kenna's parents, Uncle Jimi, Ms. Kochiyama, Mr. Rashid, Mal's abuela, the women at the safe house . . . I never knew their names, but I'll always remember their pleading eyes.

Over and over I say their names. These people whom the Other 49 have taken from me. They are the people I am fighting for. They are the people I am going back for.

No one believed I would make it to this day. My commanders laughed in my face on the first day of boot camp.

"I give her until lunch!" they roared.

"Nah, she's small but tough. Four days and she taps out!" the nice one said.

They were right. I am small. And I had to become tough. Everyone around me was stronger, bigger, and older, but I had something they didn't have.

A year ago, I was living with Mami and my brother, Ernie, in Vermont when the world split open. A teenager was killed by Border Patrol on the border between the United States and Mexico. Chaos broke out. Land mines exploded, killing who knows how many people. Out of the cracks of this dysfunction and hate came the Deportation Force. They started hunting anyone who was undocumented. California decided it wouldn't go along with their plans. The state stopped being part of the United States of America and became its own country, the Commonwealth of California. They told anyone who wanted sanctuary from the Deportation Force to come to their country. Mami decided we had to go. It was the only place we would be safe. But Mami didn't make it. They took her on the outskirts of Boston, and I was left to get Ernie, my eight-year-old brother, to California.

Whenever I close my eyes, I am running again. Running from that bus station where Mami was taken. Running from the grocery store near Sister Lottie's while the dogs were barking and snapping. Running to the river and throwing myself into the cold, dark unknown.

It took us thirty-six days to get from Vermont to California. But I didn't find peace in California. I tried for a few months to belong. I went to school, but I wasn't able to make friends. I was no longer interested in talking about my latest crush, or in makeup, or in choreographing dances. I joined community groups that focused on trying to save our water sources, but all I could think about were the moments the DF took my best friend, Kenna, or when they killed Tomás or, or, or. I stayed as long as I could for Ernie's sake.

I wanted to be the big sister that Ernie needed, the source of love and support that he obviously craved. But I couldn't be that. I couldn't play soccer, or help with homework, or clean up our rooms. I couldn't pretend that our life was normal.

There is nothing about this world that is normal anymore.

I tried to explain to my tía Luna and Ernie why I had to go back to the desert. I told them there were too many faces haunting me, too many unanswered questions, and too much anger.

I am filled with anger. Sometimes I feel like I am going to choke on it. My lungs are swimming in it. The only thing that calms me is my prayer . . .

Mami, Kenna, Rosa, Tomás, Volcanoman, Kenna's parents, Uncle Jimi, Ms. Kochiyama, Mr. Rashid, Mal's abuela, the women . . .

"I'm gonna bring Mami back. I swear," I told Ernie.

But he just scowled at me. "Stop," he said. "You can't promise stuff like that."

Ernie is so much older than his nine and a half years on Earth. This world has aged him too much, too fast. His chubby cheeks are gone, and his eyes dart around a lot, like he's always on the lookout, always being hunted. Was there ever really a world where we played in a schoolyard and blew on dandelion fuzz?

About a week into our time at Tía's, I realized that Ernie had these gaps in his mouth where he'd lost his baby teeth. He must've lost them while we were on the run, but he never told me because we were focused on trying to escape the DF.

Ernie and I have been through so much together. The meat truck filled with swinging carcasses where we saw a man get killed; the DF drone taking away a broken Rosa and a lifeless Tomás as we cowered in the trees. We jumped onto a moving train as it hurled toward California. We tied ourselves to the top of that train. It was the only way to not fall off. To not die. And yet I think it was my biggest mistake because it kept me from Mami.

The rope did its job too well. Holding us down when I wanted so badly to run. In the distance I saw the glints of cages, the icy-blue lights in the wrists of people who had been captured and taken by the DF. They were the disappeared, but by the miracle of luck, we found them in the desert.

The train brought us the unexpected gift of possibility. The gift of Mami. Through my binoculars, I saw her in the distance. I'm almost positive it was her. The blue light glowed in her wrist. She was chained to people in front of her and behind her. She was struggling to walk. But it was *her* walk. Her head tilted slightly to the right as if constantly questioning the world around her. Her hips swaying side to side, always in rhythm to a vallenato, a salsa, or a cumbia. It was how she walked in our apartment before the DF came, the way she moved in the kitchen as she made ajiaco, the way she paced around the barn when calves were about to be born.

There she was, alive. She was a couple of miles away, and an unfinished wall surrounded her, but I was sure it was her! And I needed to get to her.

I tried to untie the rope. But I couldn't. The train kept moving away from Mami as I picked and pulled at the knots binding us. I almost had it! I was so focused on the rope, I didn't notice the DF as they approached our train, but Ernie did. His screams crashed me back to reality. I could hear the buzzing drones flying toward us. The train slowed. The drones appeared, ready to swoop us into their claws. I stopped thinking about Mami and focused on the rope. I had to untie us.

Our freedom depended on it. My fingers worked miracles. We jumped off the train like birds taking flight for the first time. We smashed onto the ground, slid down a ravine, and ran away into the desert.

At that moment, I was forced to choose between Mami and Ernie. I had to decide between what was right in front of me and what might be in the distance.

I promised Mami I would get Ernie to California, and I did.

I promised myself I would go back and get Mami. And I will.

✖

"ON YOUR FEET!" shouts our commander. "Go, NOW! NOW! NOW!"

This is it. This is what I've been training for these past six months. The notorious and infamous S obstacle course. It was inspired by the Navy SEALs' training course back when California was part of the United States. But SOLIS made our course a million times harder. So here I am, running toward an obstacle course that is so impossibly difficult, more than half of us won't finish it. And to top it off, only the first six who cross the finish line will become Condors.

The course is made up of eighteen separate sections. Excruciating rope climbs, a one-hundred-foot cargo net wall, barbed wire tunnels, electrical walls we have to climb over, which are exact replicas of the new border walls that separate California from the Other 49. The worst obstacle is the weaver.

Its metal bars are about twenty feet off the ground, and we must weave our bodies in and out without falling, all the while making sure we don't touch the poison thorns strategically placed on the bars. Good news is the thorns won't kill you. Bad news is, if you touch them, the sting is so unbearable there's no way you'll finish.

The S course is complete hell on your body. It's designed to make your heart rate spike in seconds, burn out all your muscles, tap into every irrational fear you have. A small mistake might break your bones, paralyze, or kill you. It's the ultimate test. If your mind and body can handle this, then you can go into enemy territory and not only survive but finish your mission.

Every part of this course terrifies me, and yet I know it's the only way.

THE WALL

I pull myself up the cargo wall. Before I know it, I'm halfway there, fifty feet above the ground. My size is an asset as I climb. I'm light and fast; the rope doesn't buckle under my weight. I'm like Spider-Man making my way up a building, while the big guys are like clumsy bears. They ram their feet into the holes and get stuck in the netting. Their bodies splay out like eagle wings. They cuss and scream at themselves as I pass them. I can't hide my smile. It feels good to prove them wrong. I knew nothing would stop me from going back to the Other 49, to the desert, to my mami.

THE WATER

A Condor must be an expert in the water. We must be able to accomplish our missions no matter where they take us—oceans, rivers, deserts, or battlefields. I jump into the ice-cold water. My hands are bound behind my back, and my legs are taped together at my ankles. I slowly sink to the bottom of the pool. I have to fight against the instinct to kick, to squirm, to scream. My heart starts to race. My chest constricts. It doesn't matter how many times I've done this, my body always panics. It thinks it's drowning in the Colorado River. I get pulled back into memory. I see the bullets passing me in the water. My lungs burn for air. I'm counting strokes. I'm hurrying Ernie away from the DF. I have to quiet my mind. I'm not back there. I'm here in the S course. Trying to become a Condor.

My feet touch the bottom of the pool. I bend my knees and push off the ground toward the sky as hard as I can. I break through the water and inhale gulps of air. It feels so good to breathe. The sweetness doesn't last long, though. I sink underwater again, searching for the bottom of the pool with my feet. My mind focuses on what I must do—forty sinks, forty jumps. I don't count. I list my names instead.

Mami, Kenna, Rosa, Tomás, Volcanoman, Kenna's parents, Uncle Jimi, Ms. Kochiyama, Mr. Rashid, Mal's abuela, the women . . .

I try to think about the lives that each of these people lived. The love they had inside of them. I think about their dreams.

How Tomás told me he wanted to see the ocean. I think about the ocean now, and what it means to the Commonwealth of California.

California is desalinating the Pacific Ocean so we have enough water to drink, water the crops, and live. But we can only take so much water from the oceans before it becomes catastrophic. In California we recycle every drop of water. Toilet water becomes irrigation water. Shower water becomes cooking water. Leaky faucets do not exist in the Commonwealth of California. Every speck of grass in Southern California is gone, replaced with plants that are meant to live in the desert. We all understand these are small gestures and our water crisis won't be fixed this way. The only way we will survive as a country and as a planet is if we figure out how to stop climate change.

Of course, all the scientists and governments of the world can't seem to figure out how to reverse the damage done. So instead, they're determined to control the weather patterns. This is the world we live in today. A world where every single country is in a race to control the weather so they can ensure their citizens have enough water.

The news gives us water updates every day. It tells us about the race and makes it clear that the Other 49 seems to be winning, which would be dire, especially for California. If the Other 49 wins the race, it's almost guaranteed they will find a way to force us back into the union or maybe even obliterate us.

THE QUIET

This is my last test. I have no idea where I stand in the competition. I don't know if the first six have already finished and it's all over, or if I still have a chance to become a Condor. I push the thought out of my mind. I can only concentrate on where I am right now.

I slither on my stomach through mud and leaves toward my target. I find a clear spot through the bushes to take my shot. There is a white circle the size of an apple painted onto the trunk of a tree. I only get one chance to hit the target. If I miss, I fail. If I hit it, I still have to get away without being spotted by my commanders. If they see me, I fail. I aim my rifle and squeeze the trigger slowly and deliberately. I hit the shot, just off the center. It's not perfect, but it will do. I see my commanders zip around. They have no idea where I am. They're searching, but they can't see me. I press my body and face into the dirt. I'm completely camouflaged. I don't move for forty-five minutes. I need to finish in the top six, but if I'm not patient I won't finish at all. My commanders get distracted by someone else's shot. This is my moment; I don't make a sound. It's like I was never there, just how I like it.

I return to where we began the race. In the center of the large clearing is a bell. I ring it to announce I've completed my mission. I'm so tired, I want to collapse. But I can't. This final ritual has been ingrained in us. We must stay standing until we find out our placement, until we find out if we are good enough to fight as a Condor for the Commonwealth of California.

General Vargas of the Special Ops team approaches me. I can't read her face. She's like a block of stone with no emotion. Her hair is pulled back in a tight bun. Her dark black sunglasses hide her eyes. I breathe to ground myself.

"At ease, González."

She stares into my eyes. Silence. I can't stand this. I'm going to break open.

Mami, Kenna, Rosa, Tomás, Volcanoman . . .

"Valentina González, you are Special Ops number four. You're secured."

My knees buckle, but I catch myself before I fall. Tears stream down my cheeks. I wipe them away, my hands shaking uncontrollably. I want to hug her. I want to scream. I want to dance. But I can't. I just stand there trying not to burst. General Vargas leans toward me.

"Your mother would be proud," she whispers.

She places her hand on my shoulder. I look her in the eyes, unable to stop my tears. I am not surprised she knows about Mami. They know everything about us. Becoming a Condor means there are no secrets between me and my government. General Vargas turns on her heels and walks away.

Mami will *be proud,* I correct her in my head.

JESS

3:30 A.M.: The first sirens tear through whatever shreds of sleep I've found. I'm crammed into the corner of the cage, sitting up, muddling in and out of nightmares. Or maybe it's reality—I have no idea anymore. It's still pitch black in here, but clearly the sirens mean *Rise and shine!* Everyone else in the cage starts stretching and shuffling around (without saying a word to me, of course).

4:00 A.M.: All the tents have to be cleared out, and everyone has to line up at the main flagpole for roll call and the anthem, followed by a public display of depravity where maybe a dozen of the prisoners here are put into a cage and dangled over the mining pit so they can be sprayed with fake rain. Is this aqualinium in liquid form? I have no idea. All I know is it looks like it's burning people alive. I can't even watch.

4:30 A.M.: Two DF officers toss a few loaves of moldy bread at the crowd and then stand on one of their metal platforms, watching everyone claw and tear at the food. I'm cramped and woozy with hunger, but more than that, I'm still stunned by the people that were just tortured in front of us, now being carted away.

5:00 A.M.: Another series of sirens. Everyone scatters to their work assignments on cue. Two huge cages are loaded up and lowered into the mine. I'm not sure whether to get in line and pretend I'm part of the next crew, or wait for my orders. I have no idea what kind of torture the DF has planned for me around here.

"Oopsy daisy. Did someone forget about our guest of honor?" One of the officers clamps a hand around my elbow and pulls me toward a tent with a red cross on it. "Don't worry, we picked out a special job just for you," he says, chuckling through his face mask. "You're gonna help the sickos in the medical tent."

I start gagging as soon as we walk into the "medical" tent. The stench is so intense, I literally try to run back outside just to grab one more breath of fresh air.

"Ah, nope!" The officer catches me just below my ribs and throws me back in. "You'll get used to it. Or not. But either way, you're here." Then he shouts, "Incoming!" before leaving me there. I hear him zip up the tent flap, then start talking and laughing with whoever else is stationed outside.

This place is beyond gruesome. There's a row of metal folding chairs where prisoners are slumped over, moaning, shaking, cradling limp-looking children or dangling limbs in their laps. One man is hacking a lung out into a paper bag. There's a surveillance camera in every corner and not a single window or vent. After a while, another tent flap opens behind the counter and a DF officer comes out. Again, I can just see eyes through a full-face mask, but I'm pretty sure this one is a woman once she starts talking.

"You Sullivan?" she barks at me. "Let's go! This one's done."

This one is a body in the next room. A corpse now. Lying on a metal table, bloated from starvation, with too many gaping wounds to be put back together. There are a few pieces of surgical equipment lying on a counter nearby and blood staining the dirt floor. I don't even have time to run out of the room before I heave.

"Jesus Christ!" says the officer. "Seriously? Mop it up and get this one out to the back. I don't have time for this."

She disappears through another tent flap, and someone else comes out to hand me a gray mop. No water; no soap. Just a mop. When I'm done smearing my own sick on the floor, this other officer—also in head-to-toe covering, with only their eyes showing, so I have no idea if it's a person or a robot for that matter—takes one end of the gurney and motions for me to take the other. Then we wheel the dead body through the back of the tent, where there's a truck-sized pit. I'm pretty sure I see an arm sticking out, but I'm definitely not getting any closer to find out if I'm right. The officer on the other end of the gurney tips the metal top, and the body we just wheeled out slides off into the pit. I shudder hearing the thud of bones clacking together and hitting rock.

Then the woman in charge here reappears in the tent's opening.

"Back to work. Empty the buckets in the main clinic."

She points toward another section of the tent. As I walk in, my eyes start watering from the foul funk. There are two rows of beds and a single bulb hanging over them. In between the beds there are buckets full of every kind of human waste. People are sprawled out on paper-thin mattresses, on the floor, huddled in corners. They are groaning and weeping, begging for medicine or water. I've never seen anything like this level of human suffering; I don't dare look too closely. But still, I can't help but see. There's a short man whose skin is completely covered in oozing sores, a woman thrashing around like a fish out of water. There are seeping bedsheets and sunken cheeks and bodies so close to gone that I have no idea what is keeping them on Earth anymore. It's cruel that they're even alive.

I try to just focus on the task at hand. But as soon as I reach the first bucket, I get sick again. There's no way I'm going to make it through a whole day of this. I'm already so weak from dry heaving that I have to stop and put my head between my knees to find my breath. I guess it looks like I'm praying or something, because someone whispers at me, "Yes, please pray for me too."

And then a bunch more of them chime in.

"¡Un Padre Nuestro!"

"Psalm twenty-three!"

I feel like these half-dead people are using me as a prayer hotline, calling in their last requests. I don't know what to do. I want to make it clear that I have no direct connection to Jesus, or Allah, or anyone. I can't even save myself! The worst is seeing the people lying in their beds, trying to open their mouths to shout some prayer to me but not able to form words. Their voices are just raspy gurgles. Their faces are burnt or peeling. I can't help them. I can't help any of them.

One woman is flapping her arms and motioning for me to come nearer. She has huge blisters climbing up her face, and her lips are so swollen I think they might burst. The last thing I want to do is be near her.

"Please! One minute. Please!"

I inch just a little bit closer so she'll stop yelling.

"Yes?"

"Tell Ta-reek isss okay," she says.

"Tell Ta-who?"

"Ta . . . reek," she repeats. "Tarek."

"Okay," I say, nodding. She grabs my wrist. Her hand feels like a hot water balloon; her face is so close to mine, I can see streaks of infection swirling under her damp skin.

"Tell. Him," she demands.

"Yes, I'll tell him. I promise." It's a complete lie, of course. Tareek or Tarek is probably dead by now too, or at least wishes he was. The blistered woman releases her grip and falls back on her bare mattress. "Tarek, Tarek," she keeps muttering as I walk away.

"You done?" The female DF is back again, pulling thick rubber gloves off and throwing them on the ground. "Cuz I need you to strap this one down."

"Strap . . . down?"

She leads me into the operating room, where there's a new patient on the gurney. It's a woman who's been badly burned and won't lie still. Her face is so charred, she can't even open her mouth. She tosses and turns as if she's trying to flop her way to freedom. The DF officer hands me thick cloth straps so I can get the patient tied to the table, but every time I try, she shrieks, so I let the straps dangle while I stand over her. Hopefully I'm menacing enough to keep her still. Meanwhile, the officer pulls out some disgusting-looking instrument that's maybe a forceps, and I squeeze my eyes shut. Still, I can hear her peeling away the patient's burnt skin. I can feel the terror climbing up through the patient's bones, and I start trembling too. I never knew it could hurt this much to feel someone else's misery. The shuddering and writhing, the deep, wrenching moans are too much. The patient must realize there's nothing cinching her to the table. She catapults herself off and sort of melts to the ground.

"Are you kidding me?!" the officer slaps the side of my head. Then she lunges at the patient and shoves her onto the table again.

"This is your last chance!" the officer warns me.

"But . . . I can't," I whimper. "I just . . . can't."

That's it. The officer is done playing around. Without

even acknowledging me, she presses some button on the wall behind her, and in a few seconds there are three more DF officers charging into the tent, moving toward me like ravenous dogs. One of them clocks me with a fist. Another goes right for my gut. The third pushes me to the ground. I feel the packed dirt smacking my jaw, and my mouth fills with blood.

One of the officers is kicking me in the kidneys now. The tighter I curl into a ball, the harder his boot lands. I try to bury my face into the ground. I just want to dig a hole and tunnel my way out of this world. I beg them to stop, but the blows keep coming.

Until a new voice cuts in. "Okay, okay. Enough!"

Not a new voice, actually. Not new at all.

I pick my head up so quickly, everything starts spinning. But as the world comes into focus, I see him clear as day.

It's my brother, Nick.

His turquoise eyes are peering out at me through that panel in his face mask. I was always jealous of Nick's eyes. They were especially bright whenever we'd been running up through the hills or visiting Nana and Pops, where they kept the thermostat set to boiling. Nick's eyes could also hold so much rage. Sparks and daggers could fly out of them when he was mad.

"Sullivan?" he asks. "That you?"

I'm not sure how to respond. This is maybe the most humiliating and heartbreaking part of it all. Because I can see his eyes, but I have no way to get inside them. I have no way to find who we were to each other once. Sure, when we were kids he used to bully me, but we also had fun together—especially when we banded together against Mom. We once stole a pack of her cigarettes and made a bonfire in the street. He taught me how to play gin rummy, and I showed him where I kept my secret pictures of Dad. One time, Nick and I saw a Spider-Man movie together, and he shared his popcorn and held my hand during the scary parts.

But none of these things can save me now. Only Nick can. Or really, only this person inside Nick's body who's standing over me, determining my fate. There are so many layers between who we were to each other when he said goodbye and left for his first day of training, and now, with his heel inches from my hip, ready to strike.

I don't know if I'm his little sister or his prisoner.

He tips his head to one side and scowls. "I said, *that you*?"

He leans down and pokes my shoulder, which somehow makes my eyes start filling with tears. Damnit. It's not even that he hurt me. It's just that his hands and his eyes and the smell of his sweat is all so damn familiar. And he's just hovering over me, waiting for me to make the next move.

I try to say yes, but it comes out more like "Yuh."

"*Yuh*," he mimics, getting his DF cronies to laugh along with him. "You know, when they first told me about that shit you pulled in the desert, I was like, *Nah. She'd never do something like that. She'd never BETRAY our cause and let illegals go!* Because I could not even imagine you being that *idiotic*. That *pathetic*."

He lifts up my body with the toe of his boot and lets me crash back to the ground for emphasis.

"But then I paid you a little visit down at headquarters in the holding cell . . ." he continues. "Do you remember that? You were pretty out of it. Lost a lot of blood. Covered in your own shit. Not pretty. But I knew you could hear me, cuz I said, *Jessy, Jessy, why you so messy?*"

That eerie singsong is the worst. Nick hadn't done that since we were in grade school, probably. It's a little ditty he came up with when we used to play hide-and-seek. He knew it drove me crazy. His voice was always warbly and off-key, creeping me out. As Nick gets louder now, I wince without even meaning to.

"Yeah, yeah, you did that same thing. You scrunched up your face and squirmed, and that's how I knew it was definitely you," he says. "And that you weren't dead. Yet."

He gives me a good kick in the ribs to punctuate that last point. One of the other officers asks if they can join in or cart me off, and I'm trying to piece together what their plans are for me, but I also need to figure out what Nick just said about paying me a visit at headquarters. So he must've witnessed me getting tortured and beaten. Maybe even joined in the punishments or prepared my bullshit "trial."

"Aw man," Nick pouts, his voice dripping with fake sadness. "That was rough on me, Jess. I went to bat for you. I was like, there's no way she just let three illegals go. I mean, how could my sister—my *super-smart, all-honors-classes* sister—be such a fuck-up? Am I right?" His boot smashes into my stomach, and I try not to make a sound.

I hate this person so much. This loping monster who grew up alongside me, who chews with his mouth open and doesn't know how to tie his own tie but somehow thinks he can torment and humiliate me until I break. I don't know why he's keeping me alive. I can't even look at him. Clearly, whoever we were to each other doesn't matter at this point. I just have to think of him like anyone else in a DF jacket: a vicious idiot. No, a predator.

"So why'd you do it?" Nick asks. "Here's your chance to explain. Why'd you let those fuckers go?"

I refuse to answer. I'm done playing this game. Nick kicks me again, harder this time. I forgot how much he hates when I go quiet. He can't stand a fight to be over without being declared the champion. But I won't give him that satisfaction. I tuck myself into a tighter ball and let him kick and kick and kick. I try to picture Mom watching us—her eldest son driving a steel-toed boot into the back of her daughter. Is this what she wanted? Is this somehow protecting the New American Republic?

"Fine!" Nick shouts, rolling me over and yanking me to my feet. Or at least I think that's what he's trying to do, but my legs buckle and I sort of tumble into his arms. It's dangerously close to a hug.

"Jesus!" he growls. "Stand *up*!"

As soon as I get my balance, he takes his hands off me and steps back so that he's flanked by his DF buddies. He folds his arms and clears his throat too, I guess to show that he's in charge of this situation.

"Listen, I'm trying to be nice. But you're making it very difficult, *Jess*," he says.

"I'm sorry to hear that, *Nick*."

He blinks quickly. He wasn't expecting that boldness. To be honest, neither was I. But I have nothing to lose. The searing pain is radiating out to my entire torso; I can feel my left cheek blowing up to the size of a grapefruit, and I have something dripping down the leg of my pants. I'm sure it's a beautiful sight. I don't care. I do my best to stand up taller and wipe whatever blood and snot is still on my face so I can look at Nick straight on. And so he'll have to look at me. At my swollen, bruised, battered body.

It's like one of our old staring contests. We had them every morning over our Frosted Flakes or when Mom said one of us had to take out the trash. Only this time, there's a small posse of fully-armed officers behind Nick. A sea of gray ready to charge on his behalf. One of the guys even steps forward with his AK-87 raised, but Nick puts out a hand to stop him.

"Nah, it's okay," Nick says. "She's pathetic." He forces out a disgusted laugh. His buddies snort, muttering about all the cruel things they'd do to me if I was one of *their* sisters.

"I know, I know," Nick tells them. "I mean, I'm only keeping her alive because of my mom. I think she'd be kinda torn up if she got a body bag for Christmas. Then again, who knows? Maybe it'd be a relief." He cocks his head to one side. "What do you think, Mess?"

When I don't answer, he lunges at me and tugs my ponytail. It's so juvenile, but it still hurts. Every inch of my body hurts.

"Pathetic," Nick repeats. "Get back to work, you piece of shit." He turns to leave and then stops to deliver one last declaration. "Oh, and Jess," he says, "if I get any more complaints about my little sister refusing to work, I'll let one of them handle it." He nods at the DF who just raised his gun at me. "Less messy."

Nick's eyes get tiny as he laughs, so pleased with his joke.

✖

I HAVE NO idea how I make it through the rest of the day. I can't see out of my left eye, I'm pretty sure I have a cracked rib, and this uniform-sack-thing I'm wearing is soaked in blood. But I guess I'm alive enough to be of some use to the officer in charge of this "medical tent." After Nick and his posse leave, she gives me about three minutes to catch my breath and spit the dirt out of my mouth. Then she makes me get back to work, strapping down patients for her "procedures" and hauling the ones who don't survive to the pit of corpses outside.

At some point, as I'm staring at that pit, everything gets crazy blurry and I'm spinning, trying to hold on to the air, but it's slipping through my fingers. I wake up a few minutes later on the ground, staring at a sludge-colored sky. I know I should get up before a DF officer or drone sees me here, but I'm so exhausted I can't figure out how. My limbs feel like cement.

"Found her." Some other beast in DF clothing comes out, grabs a corpse's shoe, and throws it at me. It smacks me in the chest, and I can't help but whimper. The officer guffaws. "Stupid moron," he says. "You know they won't just shoot you, right? You're gonna have to work for it if you wanna die."

I've never thought about how cruel humans could be until this moment. It's pathetic, but true. I'm lying on the ground, covered in blood and vomit and probably the skin of dead people, and my body feels broken in a thousand places. And yet this person standing over me—*looming* over me in his gray uniform that somehow makes him better than me and everyone here—gets to tell me when I can die?

I can't even think of how to respond. My brain feels like it's caught in a throbbing helmet of pain. The officer gives up and lets me lie there until it's time for evening roll call. Someone else in DF gear comes out—they all look the same at this point, really. They grunt at me to go to the mess hall for evening meal and to report back in better shape here tomorrow.

I can't believe that I have to imagine a tomorrow in this place.

I somehow get myself up and wobble toward the tent that smells like food. But there's a long line of starved people coiling around the entrance, and I don't think I can stand up that long. So I make my way back to the cage that I now call home. Or hell. They're both true, I guess. I don't know where else I could go at this point. I don't know where else I could possibly belong. The thing that's slowly dawning on me is that this is not temporary. I don't have anyone who's gonna get me out of here, or even someone waiting to see if I make it.

I don't have anyone. Period.

When I think of my mom standing in the carport with Gavin as I headed out to training, all I can see is that cloud of Marlboro smoke and the sneer on both their faces. They'd be so disgusted and humiliated if they knew what I'd done to get here. There's no way they'd let me come back.

And I don't think I'd want to, anyway.

RANIA

At the mess hall that night, Isa asks me when we can do the special espectáculo. Before I can answer, Kenna chimes in, "Tonight! In one hour! Don't be late!"

Isa smiles so wide that my cheeks hurt just looking at her.

Isa was moved into our cage a few months ago. She was a tiny thing with frizzy dark braids and a birthmark that looked like a heart by her left ear. I think she's from Ecuador. Isa always slept on a metal pallet near mine, and when I asked her how old she was, she held up six fingers. She and the other young children were forced to clean the DF officers' barracks during the day, which I guess was a little less brutal than mining. But they still came back to the cages at night bleary and starving.

Isa had no mother or adult looking after her here. I didn't know if she came here by herself or if whoever was watching out for her was killed. I wanted to tell her that I was an orphan now too. That it hurt more than anything no matter how old you were or when you said goodbye. But Isa didn't speak much when I first met her. At night, she usually curled up next to Liliana, who stroked her hair until she fell asleep. When that didn't work, Kenna sang lullabies to her. Every once in a while, Isa tried to hum along. And after we were sure she was asleep, I heard a tiny whisper:

"Thank you, Señorita Kenna," and I had to choke back tears. Because even packed fifty to a cage, we were each so horribly alone.

One night, a few weeks ago, Isa came up to me and started taking off her thin sack that we all were required to wear.

"No, no," I told her. "What are you doing?" She was so skinny. We all were. Her ribs poked out like a skeleton's. But Isa wouldn't stop. She wriggled out of her sack and handed it to me.

"I'm Isa," she said with a shy grin.

I didn't know what she meant until she pointed to the inside of the sack. And there, along the worn seam at the collar, was written in spidery lettering:

Isabel Zambrano . . . Please take care of this child. She is a good child. She obeys the rules. She loves to listen to stories. She is my everything. Blessings to all!

"My mami wrote this," Isa explained. "But I can't read all of it."

"Okay," I said, trying to put the pieces together. "And you're Isabel?"

"Yes!!" she said, beaming as if I'd just brought her the sun. She pointed again to the words her mom had written and tried sounding them out. I imagined her mother working so hard to get these words down. I wondered where she got the pen. Or the strength and foresight to do this. Where did she go? Was she murdered here in a harvest? Did Isabel watch the whole thing happen?

"She's a good child," the little girl said, showing me the message again and running her finger along the words.

"Isa*bel*," I said.

"No. Isa," she corrected me.

"Okay." Then she waited for me to sound out the rest of the words with her. She read it again and again until she had it down pat. Her favorite part was definitely the *Blessings to all!* at the end. After about the tenth time, she gave me a high five that was loud and triumphant.

"¡Wepa!" she cheered.

"¡Wepa!" I echoed.

The next night, Isa was standing over my pallet when I came back from our evening "meal." She had a little boy with her; he couldn't have been more than three. Again, Isa took off her sack and read her note to me. Her voice was loud and sure. The little boy was clearly impressed. He pulled off his sack and handed it to me too.

"Tell," he said. "About Esteban." There were no words in his clothes. There was just dirt and dust and the faint smell of dried pee.

"Esteban," Isa told me, as if I needed a reminder.

“Yes, thank you. Esteban,” I said. They were both looking at me expectantly even though there was nothing else to read. So I decided to make up a story to tell them instead.

“Once upon a time, there was a boy named Esteban who lived in . . .”

“Chile!” Esteban added.

“Chile. Yes, and he loved . . .”

“Empanadas de pino!”

Isa was delighted and started to giggle.

Some of the other children in our cage must’ve heard what was going on, so they started inching toward us. Every time I paused, someone else would call out an idea to add to Esteban’s tale. They gave him a whole new adventurous life with lots of twists and turns. By the end of the story, Esteban lived in Chile with five purple horses, three chickens, two goats, his very own rainbow, and a soccer field made of bubble gum. He was thrilled.

After that, a growing group of children started coming over to my sleeping area each evening after our final roll call. We made up stories together, and Kenna taught them nursery rhymes and songs. At first, some of the mothers looked over at us nervously to see what was going on, but I told them it was okay. I knew they had to be a thousand times more exhausted, trying to take care of a child or children when they were being tortured and worked to the bone too. These women looked like ghosts.

"*Ghost* starts with *GUH*," Esteban told me.

"It starts with *G*!" Isa jumped in.

Kenna was the one who gave me the idea of actually turning this new ritual into a kind of escuela. One night, when we were with the kids, she sat on the dirt floor and started scraping out all the letters of the English alphabet with her finger, pronouncing them carefully. The kids gasped as if she was a magician. Then they each took a turn running their fingers over her writing, tracing her letters. We went through the alphabet night after night, until one of the moms told the children to give us some space. Which I did appreciate, but after a few nights, Kenna and I agreed we both needed escuela as much as they did. It gave us something to focus on or dream about when everything else just felt so unbearable.

After a week, I started teaching math to them—mostly simple addition and subtraction. We etched sentences into the dirt, and Liliana helped them draw self-portraits. One time, we took the letters from our names and made each one start a different line of poetry. My masterpiece to get them going went like this:

R: Really happy when I get to do escuela.
A: All of the people here make me smile.
N: No one is alone.
I: I can't wait to have ice cream again
A: And again!

The kids were so excited. Even little Mishi, who only had patches of hair and usually just watched us while she sucked her thumb. Mishi's mother had explained that Mishi had trouble hearing, but that she wanted to join us anyway. So the other kids decided to act out their poems and stories for her. Before I knew it, they were planning a little performance for the entire cage. They each wanted to recite a poem or story for everyone and asked me to tell them where to stand. This was going to be their special espectáculo. Tonight.

After another sleepless night with Kenna's coughing and this morning's brutal harvest, I have to admit I was planning to postpone the performance and maybe ask Liliana for an extra-long prayer circle instead. But now that Kenna has said yes, there's no turning back.

When we return from the inedible food in the mess hall, there is a clump of kids directing everyone in our cage to sit in different places. Isa is definitely in charge, trying to make space in the middle for the "stage."

"Can you sing the 'Eh Soom Boo' song at the end?" she asks Kenna. It's more like a command, coming from Isa—followed by a winning smile, of course. Kenna has taught some of the kids a few Nigerian folk songs that she loves, and Isa has memorized the words. I can tell Kenna is about to answer yes, but she gets caught off guard by another coughing fit. I know she's been trying hard all day to hold it in so none of the DF officers see her hacking up a lung. And I know she doesn't want to scare any of the kids either. But it's clear these bouts are getting more and more intense. I hate the sounds coming out of her—guttural barks that won't let up.

"Just start. Go ahead, and we'll sing something, I'm sure," I tell Isa. I really want her to move on and stop staring at Kenna.

"Okay, everybody!" Isa declares. She stands in the middle of the cage and clears her throat to get everyone's attention. Which is easier said than done, of course, since so many of us are hurting or just need to lie down. But I'm proud of the way Isa holds her own and waits for people to give her their focus.

Liliana claps her hands loudly and makes it official. "Let's have some fun, please! Isa, go ahead with your espectáculo!"

"Okay! I'll go first. We will share the poems we made in school with Señorita Rania and Señorita Kenna. Ready?"

When we all answer "Ready," she looks so excited I think she might burst. Then she says in her loudest voice, "I-S-A. Isa is my name. Don't wear it out. I know how to have fun, sing, and shout. I am a good girl. I follow the rules. Isa is my name. I am not a fool."

She does a little hip wiggle at the end to show she's done, and many people in the cage give her wild applause as she bows.

Esteban is next. He draws a lopsided *E* on the ground.

"Esteban is my name," he announces. "E-S-T-E-B-A-N. I am very good at soccer and jumping. One day I'll go back to Chile and eat a lot of cheese. Esteban."

"Esteban!" the kids respond.

Then it's Mishi's turn. I feel goose bumps climb up my

arms and legs. I know she is nervous, and I just want her to feel proud of herself even if she stands there like a statue the entire time.

"Mishi!" she shouts. "It is me!"

"Mishi!" cheer the kids in unison. Mishi is so happy, she starts hopping up and down. A few more of the kids share poems. One even does a little dance. And at the end, Isa gets back up and says, "Thank you, thank you! We hope you liked our espectáculo. We worked very hard. And we will keep on learning. Thank you most to Señorita Rania and Señorita Kenna!"

The kids are stomping their feet and clapping again. Many of the adults are cheering too. Kenna reaches for my hand and squeezes it, whispering in my ear, "I'd like to thank the Academy . . ." I feel my face and neck get all hot, but I'm so grateful to laugh instead of dissolving into tears. Then Isa runs over to us and presents both Kenna and me with bracelets that she must've made out of pieces of shoelace.

"It is from all of us," she announces.

"Thank you," I say. "It's really beautiful." The bracelet is brownish gray and has just wisps of thread holding it together, but I truly mean it. It feels like my most prized possession.

Kenna leans in and kisses me just next to my ear. I feel tears spring to my eyes because it's all so much at once. There are so many warm, expectant faces in front of us—some burned and scarred, some edging toward death already. All of us, part of some cruel human experiment. And yet, this moment is the nearest thing to joy I've felt in so long. It feels pure and untouchable, like a single blade of grass rising up in the desert.

"Maybe now we join in prayer?" Liliana offers. She holds out her hand, and Isa takes it. Then Mishi takes Isa's and waves for her mom to join her. One by one, we form our familiar circle. Liliana leads us all in a prayer that she loves. Most of us are familiar with the words by now. Then a woman I don't know as well offers a song in Creole that rumbles up from her gut and makes us all bat away tears. And then Liliana starts naming all the people we've lost from our cage—either from the harvests or from the relentless digging, the starvation and stinging dust that is slowly killing us all.

We each add names that are important to us. Sometimes our voices fall on top of each other; sometimes there is a gulley of grief that is louder than any words. When I say my parents' names, Kenna rubs my back. Then she lists her mother, father, and two missing brothers, and I lean my cheek into her shoulder, trying to absorb some of her ache. But she's consumed with another spell of coughing and retreats from the circle to catch her breath again.

"What about a prayer for the hurting?" asks Isa.

Liliana puts her hand to her heart.

"Yes," says Liliana. "This is lovely. Do you have one you want to say?"

Isa twists a few strands of her hair around her finger and looks at the ground, suddenly awkward and shy again. She used to do this all the time before we started escuela.

"Well, I hope Señorita Kenna stops coughing, please."

"It's okay! I'm okay!" Kenna wheezes.

"Yes, yes," Liliana says. "Let us send healing breath to our dear Kenna." She pauses to breathe deeply, and many of us copy her before she continues. "Does anyone else want to add a prayer? Or the name of someone in need of healing?"

People start speaking, tentatively at first. I cannot understand all the words because they are quiet and heavy with worry. Somehow it feels more hopeless to talk about the people who are ailing, who might have a chance at living. The dead at least know they're safe.

"What about her?" shouts Mishi. All eyes turn to the tiny girl's finger pointing at a huddled figure in the corner. It's the white girl from the night before. At least I think it is. She looks almost unrecognizable, covered in a mess of dried blood and bruises. One side of her face is so puffy her lips can't close.

There are a few audible gasps from the other women. Whatever we thought or assumed about her, it's clear that she's hurting now too.

"Yes, let us say a prayer for her," Liliana says. "For all those who might be hurting."

And so we do. At least those of us left standing do.

JESS

I am clinging to the cage bars, lapsing in and out of consciousness, when I hear people shuffling in—coughing, sighing, moaning. There is a little girl talking about putting on a show and ordering everyone to get in their places. I feel tears leaking out of my eyes because her voice is so light and hopeful. And everyone around her claps. Maybe this is a dream? Then I see Walter Winnecut, the man I killed in the desert. He's splayed out in a pool of his own blood, and I'm the one clapping. Applauding and cheering as his entrails fall out. It's amazing how much blood is contained in the human body. How could he hold that much in his tiny head? How could it spill out of his ears, his nose, his mouth all at once? I think I'm going to be sick just thinking about him again: the way he crept up in the dark. The way I kept pulling the trigger, riddling his body with bullets. I don't know why I didn't stop when I could see he was harmless. I just kept shooting and shooting until his blood was everywhere. Everywhere except inside him.

Noooo, please nooooo.

I think I've just moaned myself awake. There is a circle of women gazing at me. A tiny girl with patches of hair is inches from my face, pointing. I'm not sure what is going on. A few people gasp and stare. I see the two girls who are always together. They're holding on to each other like I'm some demon. They're both about my age, from what I can tell. The smaller one is named Rania, I think. The tall one has an incredible voice. She's also coughing horribly, though, and I watch them climb into a pallet together, holding hands.

Maybe they're clinging to each other because they're lesbians—which I thought would disgust me. At least it would have before I got here, but now, as I look at their skinny arms intertwined and the little matching shoelaces around their wrists, my eyes start to pool with tears. I know it's stupid, but I've never had anyone who wanted to hold my hand like that. And now I don't know that I ever will. I'm afraid for tomorrow to come. I'm afraid for whatever torture is inside tonight. I'm afraid to even try to move my body or lick my cracked lips.

But that older woman who led the prayer circle—the one with deep, kind eyes and a little limp—she is here now, inching toward me. Maybe she's not that old actually. Maybe it's just the weight of all this suffering and torture that ages her. As I watch her come closer, I see that her eyes are dark and wondering. She doesn't say a word, just looks over my crumpled body and sighs. She puts one hand on my wrist, and I yelp involuntarily.

"Shhh, shhh," the woman says. Her hands are warm and dry. She brushes back my matted hair and lifts up my bloody palms to inspect them. "My name is Liliana. I am going to help you, okay?"

I try to nod and mumble some sort of thank-you. My mouth is so swollen that I'm not forming words well.

"Just one moment," Liliana says. I follow her with my one open eye as she goes to her bed, retrieves something from under her blanket, and starts toward me again. Then she lifts up a little cloth and presses it to my cheek. It's soft and worn and somehow cool. My whole body shivers with pain, but I don't dare stop her.

"It's okay," she tells me. "I'm making it clean." I don't know why she's doing this. It hurts like hell, but it's also one of the nicest things I think anyone's ever done for me. Liliana pats the cloth on my other cheek, then down on my neck. I hear her humming something low under her breath as she travels across my chin, and I can't help it—I start ugly crying, snuffling, and whining.

"I'm sorry," I whimper.

She shakes her head and continues cleaning my body ever so gently. "It's okay," she whispers.

"No, no, it's not." I feel a stabbing sensation in my right ribs every time I try to talk, but I need to tell her. "It's not okay. It's not what I thought . . ."

Maybe she doesn't understand me. Or she does and she doesn't believe me. They all know I'm a former DF. How could

I not know what was really going on? On some level, I *had* to; I just chose to ignore it. I drank the Kool-Aid. I pledged to uphold the sanctity of our new nation, and I raged about these parasites stealing into our homeland so they could take all our jobs. I thought the DF was going to stop all the droughts and wars and people rushing the border.

I hear the evening sirens going off, and an announcement blares from outside. Some of the women head out for the night shift in the mine. But Liliana stays right by my side.

"I'm just . . . sorry," I say again.

"Okay," she responds. I can tell that neither of us is really interested in my poor excuses. My dawning realizations aren't going to save anyone now. Especially not this cage full of women who've been brutalized and abused for far longer than I have. I have nothing to offer them, which only makes me cry more.

Liliana continues humming. When her rag gets too caked in dried blood and dirt, she wipes it on her clothes, making dark swirls on her sack thing that we're all forced to wear. Then she leans in close to me. Her breath is hot on my eyes.

"It will be all right," she says again. "We will get you better. And tomorrow, when you go back to the medical tent, I need you to do something for me."

Even the thought of going back there makes me shudder, but I've never wanted to do something for someone else more than right here, right now.

"Yes. Of course," I answer.

"You are going to get me hilo y aguja," Liliana says. She starts pantomiming what she means, with one hand lying flat and the other weaving up and down as if she is sewing.

"You mean needle and thread?" I say. She nods. "But how?"

Liliana smiles, the creases around her eyes growing thick and long.

"You're a smart girl. You will figure it out. And then we will sew you back together."

VALI

I rest my head in Malakas's lap. He runs his fingers through my hair. Every part of my body screams in agony, but being with him somehow makes the pain feel good. This morning I was just a soldier climbing up walls, crawling through tunnels, and almost drowning. Tonight, I am a Condor.

"I knew you'd get it," Malakas says. I squeeze my eyes shut, trying to hold on to this moment of calm. I am with the person who understands me completely, and I don't need to say a word. Our silence comforts me. We don't have to pretend with one another. We are our true selves always. Death came for us so many times on our way to California; now nothing but the truth lives between us.

"Have they told you when you're being deployed?" he asks me.

"No, but I think it's gonna be soon."

His eyes look off into the distance. I know this is hard for him. It's hard for me too.

Malakas joined SOLIS because of me. When I told him I was signing up, he asked if he could go with me. I wasn't expecting him to come, but I was praying he would. We started boot camp together, but Malakas was recruited into technology and analysis right away. The higher-ups instantly saw his brilliant mind would be most useful in tech development. He didn't want to leave me. We hadn't been away from each other since we met on our way to California. But we soon realized once you join SOLIS, you don't have a say about where you go or what you do.

Now that I'm a Condor, I'll leave for SOLIS's headquarters when they call me. I've been told I'll be heading back into enemy territory. The headquarters are in slot canyons in the middle of the desert. They've been there for a long time without being detected by the Other 49. I can't even begin to imagine what it looks like there, but I'm excited to find out!

The countdown with Malakas begins right now. We don't know how much time we have together, but we will make the most out of every moment. He's been my constant, my North Star, my rock for almost a year.

Malakas was born in northern Luzon. He said it was a mixture of poverty and never-ending typhoons. When he turned six, Luzon was hit with a string of deadly storms that buried his elementary school in a mudslide. The waters became contaminated, and his mother got so sick, she couldn't even swallow rice. She begged a childhood friend to help get Malakas to the United States. He moved in with his grandmother, or as he called her, his lola, in a tiny apartment in Brooklyn for the next ten years. Malakas told me about how kind and smart his lola was. He told me about getting his counterfeit chip in the back of a nail salon, and that very same night hearing that his town in Luzon had been washed away, obliterated. His mom, his home, everything he knew: gone. He kept going to school because that's what his mom would have wanted him to do.

One day, on a regular morning in Brooklyn, Malakas came back from basketball practice and his lola's apartment was completely trashed. The windows shattered. His lola was gone. She had been taken by the DF. He packed the only belongings he had left—his favorite book about the stars, his binoculars, and he started running.

Malakas was by himself for such a long time. A wandering shadow, completely alone after his lola was taken and his mother was washed away. When California seceded and announced all immigrants were welcome inside of its borders, Malakas started his journey west. We met in a meat truck among the carcasses of dead animals and undocumented people running for safety. From that day on, Malakas and I have been through everything together. It took us a little bit of time to trust one another, but once we did, we never doubted or judged each other again. We knew that together we would find safety, together we would find my mami and his lola.

Malakas eventually turned into my almost boyfriend about six months ago. I told him I couldn't imagine having a boyfriend while the world was collapsing around us. It seemed so frivolous and unfair. Frivolous because what does a boyfriend mean when there isn't enough water, and people are being disappeared into the desert, and kids are losing their parents? Unfair because how could I feel the pleasure of my first kiss when I imagined Mami was being chained and beaten? How could I have a boyfriend and not have Kenna to share my feelings with? But I didn't pull my hand away when he held it as we ate dinner. I couldn't resist kissing him. I didn't want to say no when he asked if he could take off my shirt. I couldn't let myself have a boyfriend, but I couldn't stop myself either.

Malakas presses his soft lips against mine. His kiss is both comforting and exciting. His tongue finds mine. I taste his sweetness. I want to press my body against his. I pull him onto me. His weight feels good against my tired muscles. Our bodies move in a joint rhythm. The world is so harsh around us, but his tenderness is everything I need.

Time seems to compress into itself during my final days with Malakas. I can't tell if two minutes have passed or if several days have gone by. We laugh, we cry, we dream, we eat, we make love. It is both glorious and painful. I find myself in the familiar position of choosing between what is right in front of me and what might be in the future.

We decide we are going to spend our last night together looking at the stars. I go to meet him after work. I see him talking with his coworkers. I've always been amazed by how comfortable he is in groups. When he speaks, people listen. He's kind and honest, and folks trust him because of it. He knows this about himself, and he's such a noble person, he would never use this to his advantage. He's been good to me, and I believe I have been just as good to him. He turns to me as I approach him. He smiles his beautiful, dorky, cute smile. *Damn, I'm going to miss him.* He says goodbye to his friends and takes my hand in his.

Besides us there isn't much out here. We can see the pinpricks of light from the massive wall that was built around California after it seceded. But if we position ourselves just right, with the wall behind us, we can make ourselves believe we are just normal teenagers hanging out on a regular night. The moon is glorious tonight. It's bright and full and feels as if it's promising us all the time we desire. I know it's not. We only have until sunrise. I want to say so much to Malakas, but there is nothing left to say, so I kiss him.

His lips are welcoming, and full of love. They are my parting gift. They are my parting sunset. They are my home.

✖

I'VE BEEN HIKING through the desert on our journey to SOLIS's headquarters for a few hours. We finally make it to the wall that surrounds California.

As soon as California seceded from the US, the Other 49 constructed this new monstrosity. They promised it would have electric rods shooting out of the top of it, poisonous mesh, and barbed wire twisting and undulating for miles. But they haven't been able to complete it yet. SOLIS has mapped the wall and knows exactly where we can breach it—most of the electrical rods don't have electricity running through them, and the outposts have yet to be manned. We crouch in a small irrigation tunnel on the California side and wait for nightfall. Then Anwar, our platoon leader, orders us to scale the wall with specialized suction cups that are strapped to our hands and feet.

I cannot ignore the irony of coming back to the place I risked my life to escape. I start to think about everything that has happened in the last year. This world isn't whole. It's broken in so many ways. It is burning and melting. It is hurtling toward world war. In this moment alone, there are so many reasons to mourn.

I'm a few feet above the ground. I jump off the wall and land inside the Other 49. The ground feels like it's cracking underneath us. The dredging and droughts have gotten so bad here. There are deep gashes in the earth that must be dry riverbeds; there are sinkholes as wide as houses that look like some sort of drilling exercise gone awry. As we get farther into the Arizona desert, we are surrounded by a grayish-green haze. I can just make out a tangle of felled trees and tiny mountain ridges in the distance. The smell of wildfires and burning brush is so thick. I get this bitter metallic taste in my mouth like I'm breathing in strange fumes.

A few hours after we cross, Anwar raises his hand, motioning for us to stop. No one makes a sound. We have all been trained for this. Follow orders without question. Finish your mission.

Anwar motions for us to take cover. We each pull out our foil blankets, which are covered in camouflage so we blend into the desert seamlessly. The air starts buzzing around us. My breath quickens. I cover every inch of my skin with the foil blanket. I know the drones can't detect me under this thin piece of foil. No matter how many times I've hidden from drones this way, it still unnerves me. The drones pass us by. Their radar signals bounce off our foil blankets, leaving us undetected. I still don't understand how our janky blankets can trick their technology. Malakas explained it to me once. He thought it would help my constantly racing heart. It didn't, but it did convince me to always have a foil blanket folded in my back pocket.

We wait in silence until it's safe to move. Once out from under the blankets, my eyes focus on the only thing around us: the large rock formations in the distance. A few moments later, I am able to make out a person in front of the rocks. Anwar motions for us to make our way toward the rocks. I see a tall woman with deep-set eyes, short dark curly hair, and a scar that runs from the corner of her mouth to her earlobe. Behind her is a pitch-black tunnel that snakes its way through what seems like impenetrable rock.

"Welcome to SOLIS. My name's Colonel Soujani. Come in."

We walk through the unlit tunnel. It's so dark, I can't even see my hand in front of my face. Then we turn a corner, and suddenly there is light all around us. The walls of the slot canyons stretch into the sky for what seems like miles. The thick mountain rock protects us against the enemy's radar. Colonel Soujani explains to us that above the rock there is an invisible protective shield that works almost like a mirror. It's brand-new technology that reflects the top of the slot canyons so the naked eye can't see us. It also makes any radar detection impossible. So far, the Other 49 hasn't found SOLIS's headquarters.

The canyons themselves are incredible, zigzagging all around us like a slick maze, with swirls of brown and red and even specks of gold. It has taken centuries of flash floods and erosion to carve out this place. In some spots, the rock walls are so tall, they look like they're poking through the clouds. In other places, they're just twenty feet above my head, with slashes of sunlight pouring in.

It's amazing. There is an entire society here in the slot canyons. It's a place where people sleep, eat, fight, love, live right under the nose of the Other 49. It's like a whole city. People have tents and lean-tos for sleeping; there are solar panels, generators, and two huge water filtration tanks at either end. Every inch of this space is being used. There are tents that are filled with the glow of computer screens and others that hum with hydrocurrents. Lots of people stand in circles studying holographic blueprints that hover over them. SOLIS is California's military, and California has invested heavily in it. It's clear they know California's future lies in making sure they can protect themselves against the Other 49 should there ever be a war. It's both inspiring and shocking to be here. How is it that this exists and people don't know about it? How is this secret so out in the open in enemy territory? Colonel Soujani reads my mind.

"Don't worry. You're safe here. This is the last place they'll look for us. So follow every single rule. You fuck up, you fuck our revolution. Condors, come with me," the colonel says. "Leadership council is ready for you."

Colonel Soujani walks at a very fast pace. We're tired and thirsty, but it doesn't seem to faze her that the six people following her have been walking and sleeping in the desert for days. The leadership council is waiting for us, and that is all that matters. She tells us little snippets of what is going on around us as we wind our way through canyons to a supply area where there are metal shelves full of first aid and hygiene supplies—there are half-moons of soap, baking soda pellets, and salt tablets all there for the taking. We walk through another rocky path to a huge water receptacle where people get jugs they can fill for the day. The filtration system here looks pretty phenomenal, with soft pipes twisting and turning around two ginormous tanks and then into the ground. There is also a sewage receptacle, which of course doesn't smell the greatest, but just like back home, it recycles the waste and then feeds the water back into an aquifer.

The canyons are so much bigger than I realized. They curve and stretch out as far as my eye can see, sometimes splitting into little forked paths that are so thin, we have to hug the rocks and shimmy through one at a time. After the water filtration section, we take two lefts and a right, or maybe two rights and a left, and meet a team of people who are responsible for all communications with California. There's also a team in charge of intercepting communications between the Other 49 government officials, labor camps, and the Deportation Force. There's a section of the canyons that's set up as a lab so people can study new water sources. Everyone here is kind enough, but very busy. There is a man plotting points on a large projected map, and people are bustling around. I want to figure out exactly what is going on, but the colonel steers us away.

Around another corner there's a wide platform where an agricultural team has managed to grow rows of vegetables—there's some hearty-looking cactus, some rubbery-looking kale, and even a row of corn that the colonel points at proudly.

"We grow all our food here. So eat what you're given. All of it. Always."

"Yes, ma'am!" we say in unison.

Mami never let me waste my food either. The colonel is tough, but there is something about her that I like.

I smile, missing Mami so much.

Colonel Soujani approaches a slot canyon wall. The walls have been smoothed by centuries of water, when it was abundant and humans weren't even a speck on this planet. Part of me wishes we could go back to that time, before we even began, maybe to never begin. If we were never here, we wouldn't have been able to destroy the Earth or one another. When I'm alone at night with my thoughts, this is where my mind takes me. This is where my thoughts wander.

The colonel's eyes are scanned, and a door slides open. Inside there is a large table and three people sitting down behind it. They each rise as we enter. I recognize all of them. We were briefed about the leadership council in California.

To the left is Dr. Holland. He is a small man with glasses and fingers that constantly flutter as if he's inputting everything that is being said into his mind. To the right is the Secretary of Defense. She has long red hair. It's perfectly parted down the middle and hangs to her waist. The worry lines around her mouth run deep. I wonder if she ever smiles. General Choi stands in the center. He looms large in this room. Everyone respects him. They say he is a kind and fair man. He doesn't give big speeches or make people feel small so he can feel important. The story of how he became the general of SOLIS was legend among us at boot camp.

General Choi joined the Marines when he was eighteen. He grew up in New Jersey in a mostly Korean neighborhood. He saw his parents struggle to make ends meet his entire childhood. He knew college wasn't an option for him, but he wanted to have a life outside of the restaurant where his parents worked. The Marines were the answer. He was disciplined, smart, and reliable. He rose through the ranks quickly. By the time he was forty-three years old, he was forced to make a decision that would dictate the rest of his life and that of millions of people.

In 2024, the President of the United States decided he was going to stay the President for a third term. There were protests in the streets, but not enough. Some people were outraged, but more people were happy. The President ignored the Constitution, and all the other politicians did too. But General Choi did not. He knew what the President was doing was illegal and dangerous. The day the President declared himself the winner of a third term, General Choi resigned. He wasn't quiet about it either. He was on every TV station, podcast, and radio show. He spoke honestly about how the President's actions were wrong, against the law, and morally corrupt. He encouraged people to take to the streets, to protest, to organize, to refuse to accept this man as their President. After a couple of days, the President issued a warrant for the general's arrest, charging him with treason. But by that time, SOLIS had already been in contact with him. They took him and his family to a secret SOLIS safe house. For almost a decade, he worked for SOLIS. He became so central to the resistance movement that he helped orchestrate the secession of California. And ever since then, General Choi has been one of the leaders of SOLIS, and he's now leading California's military.

My Condor squad and I salute the General.

"Take a seat, soldiers."

As we sit in our designated chairs, I feel my heart beating so loud, I'm sure everyone must hear it too. This is the only thing I have wanted (except for getting Mami back) for the past year. Most nights my dreams have been filled with all the horrors I saw from the top of that train in the desert—people in chains being beaten by the DF. The blue lights in their wrists shining bright, announcing to anyone who cares to listen that they are not free. I hear Mami calling me, crying for me, begging me to rescue her. Ever since Mami was taken from me, I hate to sleep. Today, my heart thunders inside of me because it knows I'm getting closer to her.

"Condors, it's good to have you here with us," says General Choi. "Let's get to it. You are now part of Operation Tempest. It's a two-part operation. The first part has been active for a year. Once we started hearing rumors that the people being rounded up by the DF were not being deported but rather being sent to labor camps, we started to investigate. We were able to confirm, pretty quickly, there was indeed a labor camp. We knew we needed to get someone inside right away. We created a communication system and deployed an undercover agent into the camps. In other words, she turned herself in to the DF and was taken to the camp. We owe her a lot. She sacrificed her freedom for all of us."

A 3D image of the labor camp appears hovering at the center of the table. The general swipes at the air to make the image rotate as he speaks.

"She has been instrumental in getting us the information I am about to share with you. What I am going to tell you is top secret. We have confirmed there is an aqualinium mine in Arizona." He zooms in on the image.

Aqualinium? What the hell is that? My mind races through every presentation we had at boot camp but comes up with nothing.

The image shows large holes in the ground. There is a cage hanging above one of them. The cage is packed with people. I can't see their faces, but I can clearly make out the shapes of their bodies. There are women, men, and kids. They must be mothers and fathers, children, and grandparents. They once lived in apartment buildings and in cul-de-sacs. They worked as doctors and librarians, gardeners and trash collectors. They had barbecues on Sundays with their neighbors. Maybe it was those very same neighbors who reported them to the DF.

"The mine runs twenty-four hours a day. The work day is divided into two shifts. A few thousand people work each shift. There are two hundred officers patrolling right above the mine and another three hundred throughout the camp. We don't know how many officers work inside the mine itself, but we believe there aren't many down there. We estimate about one hundred armed drones are monitoring the skies and the surrounding areas. The camp itself is fortified with electrified walls. Unlike the wall around the California border, these actually work. Dr. Holland?" The general sits down, and now Dr. Holland stands up. He swipes the image away, and another appears. This one is inside of the mine.

"Aqualinium is a delicate mineral once it's removed from its naturally occurring rock formation. We haven't been able to figure out how aqualinium can impact weather patterns yet, but we are trying. As far as we know, this is their only goal with aqualinium. We've learned that aqualinium has other benefits too. It's highly explosive in small quantities. We've been able to obtain minuscule amounts for our studies, which have been limited—but I digress. To be effective, aqualinium can only be mined by humans. They must extract the rocks with basic tools and then get the small pieces of aqualinium with their bare hands. We believe this is the reason for the camps. Prisoners' hands are the key to giving the Other 49 the ability to control the weather. We believe once they've perfected this technology, they will use it to alleviate the drought in the Other 49 and possibly various countries of their choosing. Needless to say, this amount of power would give them great influence over the entire world."

Dr. Holland continues to speak, but I don't hear his words. My legs are shaking, and I feel a ball of fire growing in my belly. It wants to burn everything down.

This sick plan of the Other 49's—rounding us up and ripping us from our families, locking us in cages and treating us like cattle—it was all for aqualinium! They said we were hurting them, that we were taking away their jobs, we were a health hazard, freeloaders, a burden to the good working citizens, blah blah blah, but really all they wanted was our free labor. A country going back to its deplorable roots. Instead of cotton killing people, it's now some crumbly rock called aqualinium.

"We have to stop them!" I blurt out.

Everyone's eyes turn to me. I know I wasn't supposed to speak, but I couldn't help myself. I don't know why we're just sitting here talking about it when there's so much to be *done*.

The general seems slightly annoyed, but he is kind in his

reply. "Yes, soldier. That's why you are here. As I said, it's a two-part operation. Our agent on the inside is figuring out how to make the mine explode. Once she knows how to do this, she will give us our go date. Your mission is as follows." The general swipes in another image. A small building appears. It's a simple one-story box. No windows and only one door.

"You will breach the labor camp walls when the mine explodes. The explosion will serve as a distraction to get you in. The officers and drones will be focused on the explosion. Plus, there will be a thousand SOLIS soldiers invading the camp to get as many people out as they possibly can. Your mission is to get inside this building. Once inside, you must log in to the computer and download every single file onto a thumb drive. As the files are downloading, a virus, which is on the thumb drive, will be released into every computer on the Other 49's internal network. This virus is programmed to destroy all information that is connected to aqualinium. After the download is complete, you must blow up the computer and everything in the building. If this is executed correctly, the virus will permanently delete everything the Other 49 knows about aqualinium.

"You won't have a lot of time to do this, but it will be enough. It is imperative to our national security that you bring us those files."

"And what will you do with the files?" I ask.

"Direct and to the point," a voice booms into the room. President Morales's image pops up where the aqualinium mine was just seconds ago. "I like you," she says to me with a smile. I smile back but don't say a word. President Morales's presence is soothing yet authoritative. She addresses the nation every night in California. Her location is always secret. Assassination attempts against her have increased with each passing day. She always exudes a sense of calm, but this past year of leadership in California has aged her. Her long black hair is now streaked with white. It's the only sign of the pressure she is under.

"As the general said, this mission is critical to the survival of our country. The files you are taking will allow us to access everything the Other 49 knows about aqualinium. We'll be able to conduct our own experiments, and eventually we'll be able to harness weather patterns. Imagine ending the drought in California. We'll be able to help our neighbors in Mexico and bring relief to the countries most in need, like Australia and South Africa. Each of you has taken on the responsibility to ensure the safety and freedom for the people of California. Aqualinium ensures this. The freedom of millions rests on your shoulders."

There's no way to know whether this plan will work. There's no way to shut out all the chatter in my brain, the what-ifs and what-nows, the swirling images of explosives and body parts flying in every direction. But I have to draw some faith from the fact that I am fighting back. I am not running away because I am no longer afraid. I'm not even afraid of death. I just can't leave this Earth before I hug Mami one more time.

RANIA

The next day, before we're split up into different parts of the mine, Kenna asks me to skip the evening meal and meet her at our hiding spot instead. Of course I say yes.

The entire day, I feel a mild jolt of adrenaline; I'm ridiculously productive too. The sulfuric stench of the mine is suffocating. The little ventilation tubes with their rickety fans just make noise and swirl the dust around more. And I have searing pains in my arms as I pick apart the aqualinium pebble by pebble. But even when I'm in the darkest tunnel in the mine, chipping away at the rocks, I have this weird momentum. Because I know there's someone I love and trust who will be there waiting for me.

The spot that Kenna and I have found is just this little patch of scrubby weeds in between the huge trash containers. It smells vile, and there's always some sort of desert rat skittering around, but it's ours. Kenna's already nestled in by the time I get there. She is curled into a tight knot, coughing as quietly as she can. I drape myself over her, trying to absorb her gasps and wheezing. It takes longer and longer for her to recover from these fits now. And yet the first thing she does once she can breathe again is pull me into her, tuck my hair behind my ear, and kiss me. I feel myself sink into her arms, melting.

"Are you ready for this?" Kenna asks.

"Yeah! What?"

"I *think* I found our escape route."

I kiss her again. She is constantly coming up with new ideas for how we're going to break out of here. I love her ingenuity, even if it feels pretty impossible.

"No," Kenna says, reading my mind. "I'm serious this time!"

"Okay! Well, where? How?!"

"Remember how I was trying to figure out where those two new outhouses came from?"

"Yes . . ."

We have about five thousand prisoners in this labor camp and a total of ten outhouses. Which is about as hideous as it sounds.

"I was curious because they were closer to the wall and didn't have any receptacles next to them. Instead, it looks like they were drilled into the ground . . ."

I'm not sure what Kenna is getting at, but she seems so hopeful that I want to follow her line of thinking.

"Don't you see?" she asks. "They must have tunnels under them. For all the . . . stuff."

"You mean . . . sewage pipes?" I almost gag just thinking about it.

"Yes," says Kenna, breathing out. "But think about it, Rania. It's perfect. If we can get down there, we'll be underground. Nobody will look for us there. And they have to dump out on the other side of the camp wall, right?"

"I . . . guess so."

I really wish I could feel her level of optimism, but I don't know how this could work.

"Just think about what's on the other side, Rania," she urges. "We'll be able to see the sky and breathe real air."

"Aaaah." I sigh. Even the thought of fresh air makes me loosen up a little.

Kenna is full-on planning our new life now. "We'll find a way to California and eat actual food," she tells me. "We can sleep on pillows and wash our clothes."

"I want to smell everything," I gush. "I want to smell cinnamon and sandalwood and even gasoline. Anything except for these rocks."

"Right?" Kenna presses my hands between hers. "We can hold each other and love each other. I want to wash your hair and feed you mangoes. We can kiss whenever and wherever we want . . ."

Then she kisses me slowly, softly. On my neck, under my ear, in my hair. It feels electrifying. I'm desperate to kiss her back, to hold her so close she can never slip away.

"Please . . ." she whispers.

I don't say yes or no. I just press my lips into hers, trying to swallow us both. Kenna takes one of my hands and puts it on her heart so I can feel it beating. *Ba-bum, ba-bum.* My whole body feels like it's thumping with hers, everything pulsing in the most breathtaking way. I creep up Kenna's arm, laying soft kisses in a trail. I kiss the scar snaking its way from the bottom of Kenna's chin to the left corner of her lips. It's a winding river cutting through her skin, and I kiss every speck of it. Touching Kenna like this is both familiar and new. When I hear her sigh, I have this overwhelming need, this hunger to be connected, our bodies becoming one.

Kenna feels it too; I can tell. We are both so turned on now. It's hard not to moan as she pulls me into her, kissing my neck, my chest, my ribs. Devouring me. A thrilling heat climbs up from the base of my spine. I am all over her now. My tongue, my lips, my hands. These hands that have been burned and poisoned, charred and scarred—I get to use them to give her pleasure. And her hands are on me, inside me, pulling me into a rush of desire. I feel us both shivering and erupting—erasing everything and everyone except us.

After we catch our breath, I burrow my head into that special spot between Kenna's ear and collarbone, and I whisper, "I wanna do *that* when we get to California."

Kenna giggles a little. "Yes, we will!"

"Like, every day. Or every other day. Or . . . whenever we can. Ooh, I want to get a bungalow, and then we can plant a lemon tree."

"Yes, yes!"

I know it sounds ridiculous. We have no idea whether there even is a California anymore, but I don't care. I have to believe in it all. I have to let it be possible.

"We *can*," says Kenna. "We *will*. C'mon. I want to show you those outhouses before the night sirens."

"Wait. Let's just sit here for a few more minutes. Please?"

Kenna is too determined, though. "I need you to see this," she says. She kisses me firmly and starts to shimmy out of our spot, as if she's going to take off for those outhouses right now.

"Hold on—" I reach for her hand, but before I can pull her back, she's stopped by deep, wracking coughs again. She's trying so hard to be quiet too. Her body is shaking and rocking with the effort of containing it all.

I guide her back into my arms and wait for the fit to pass, massaging her trembling shoulders. When she has enough air in her lungs to speak, the first words Kenna utters are: "Okay, but you promise to come look with me tomorrow?"

"Yes."

"Swear on your life?"

"I swear! And whatever life I have is yours!"

Kenna's face looks so serious as she continues speaking. "Rania, I don't think this cough is going away, and I don't have much time. The outhouses are our best option. Unless . . . you have another idea?"

She looks at me straight on, unblinking. She does not move. She does not speak. I hate this. No, I don't have any other ideas. But it doesn't mean I'm not just as desperate to get out of here.

"It's just, I don't understand," I whine. "What happens if the tunnel ends? We could suffocate down there. And if we do get to the other side, there must be DF out in the desert. Plus, the drones. The electric wall."

I keep blabbering about fears and excuses. Kenna waits for me to peter out before opening her mouth again. Her voice is low now. "I get it," she says. "But just know, we're running out of time . . ."

Her urgency feels like a windstorm, turning everything inside out. Her cough is definitely getting worse, but she's still fit enough to work. So would they call her up for the harvest? I can't imagine that. I *refuse* to imagine that. At the same time, I don't think crawling into a sewage pipe is going to save either of us.

"We're gonna make it," I tell her. My voice sounds hollow and unconvincing.

"I hope so," she answers.

"I *know* so," I tell her. "I'm going to look at the outhouses with you tomorrow and then . . . we'll make our plan. We'll get out of here."

I want to believe in this outhouse idea, even if Kenna is coughing again and the thought of her inhaling shit while we somehow crawl under the electrified wall . . . It's all so desperately improbable. I rub her back. I wait for the fit to pass. I nod as she leans in and kisses me.

"Thank you," she whispers.

"Are you . . . okay?" I ask.

Kenna smiles, tucking my hair behind my ears again. She looks lost in an untouchable sorrow. "I'm okay, Rania," she tells me. "I mean, as much as any of us can be, right?"

VALI

Breakfast is not great, but I am grateful for it. I pick at the hard piece of toast, with a tiny bit of butter slopped in the middle. Next to it is a small banana, way too ripe for my taste, and a protein bar. We don't get a lot of meat in SOLIS. It's too hard to care for animals in the slot canyons. So everyone is a vegetarian. I'm fine with it. We hardly ate meat at home anyway. Mami only splurged on chicken and meat on birthdays, graduations, and Nochebuena.

The colonel's words ring in my head.

We grow all of our food here. Eat it. All of it.

I force the banana down my throat and move on to the toast. I have a meeting with the leadership council, so I start walking toward the meeting room. I've only been there once before, and there are so many rocks and passages that split off into darkness with no warning or reason that getting lost is expected. It was suggested we use an escort until we got our bearings, but I am determined to find my way alone. I traveled across the country without even a map; I better be able to find my way through a few tunnels.

I cross into another section of the canyons. I glide my fingers against the wall. It's a nice distraction to look at my fingers skating along the rocks. Their smoothness calms me. My doubts and worries about the mission melt into the wall. By the time I get to the meeting room, I am grounded and ready.

I enter the room and sit down at the table along with the other five Condors. We wait for the leadership council to arrive. I nod at Dre, who is leading this mission. He nods back. He is very tall, very muscular, and smart. His family has been in California for generations. No one in his family was taken by the DF, but his love for California is what made him join SOLIS. Next to him is Vero. She's got tattoos all over her body. The one on her neck is the most impressive: an intricate owl face takes up the entire front part of her neck. Its wings wrap around all the way to the back of her neck. I asked her about it once, and she said, "Owls symbolize inner wisdom, change, and transformation. Everything we need for SOLIS to be successful." I have a good feeling about her. She's the only other girl on the team.

Next to me is Alan. He barely ever speaks, but he knows everything that is going on around him. He has photographic memory and is the most incredible marksman. At the end of the table sit cousins Lisifrey and Julian. They are the complete opposite of one another. Lisifrey is tall. Julian is short. Lisifrey has the strength of a lion, and Julian has the speed of a panther.

They always work as a team and are unstoppable. They both lost their entire families to the DF and want nothing more than to destroy the Other 49. My team is solid. They are the best of the best. I know they are supposed to be here. I wonder if they feel the same way about me.

General Choi bursts into the room with Colonel Soujani and Dr. Holland behind him. We jump up from our seats and salute him.

"At ease, soldiers," he says as he sits and pushes a button on the table. An image of a DF officer appears. My blood rushes to my face, and my breath quickens. I haven't seen that uniform since I got to California. I try to steady myself. My fellow Condors can't know that a picture of a DF officer sends my heart racing.

"This is the DF officer who has access to our target, Officer Belton. The only way to gain access to the building is with his chip. The chip cannot be cut out. He must be alive when the chip is scanned to open the door. As soon as he dies, the chip is deactivated."

I rub the scar on my wrist where my fake chip used to be. In the before times, when we all lived in what was still known as the United States of America but no longer the land of the free (and to be honest, it never really was), a law was passed that every citizen had to have a chip inserted into their wrist. I watched Ernie get his when he was just a baby, and he barely squeaked. It was easy, since he was born in the US. But for me and my parents, it was far from easy. We had to find someone who could give us a fake chip. When we finally found someone, it was so expensive, Mami and Papi gave every penny they had. But I got my chip. It kept me safe until the Deportation Force started hunting us.

To make it easier for the DF, the government implemented a system upgrade, and suddenly anyone with a fake chip had an ice-blue light, no bigger than a grain of rice, glowing from their wrist. Mine started to glow when Malakas, Ernie, and I were on the run to California. I knew as soon as I saw the light that it was only a matter of time before we'd have to cut it out. Malakas did it for me. I remember the sensation exactly, shooting up my arm, slicing time into before and after this moment. The knife cutting my veins and splitting me open. I saw the knife worming its way through my skin as he searched for the light. I blacked out before he got to the chip. When I woke up, my wrist was in a bandage, and his was too. I was supposed to help him cut his chip out after he cut mine out. He did his part, but I couldn't stick to my end of the bargain. Malakas did what he always does—he took care of it himself. We have matching worm scars now. A forever reminder of all we have been through together.

I rub my scar. It calms me. My heart rate begins to slow. I focus on the general's words.

"You must find Officer Belton to gain access to the location. As soon as he is secured, Valentina and Dre will take him inside. Once inside the location, he will need to have his eyes scanned to get access to the files on the computer. Do whatever you need to do to get his eyes opened so they can be scanned. Remember, he must be alive. After you gain access to the computer, you must download all the files onto the thumb drive, which will release the virus. The moment you have everything, destroy the location and the computers, and terminate the officer. Understood?"

"Yes, sir!" we say in unison.

To terminate the officer is to kill him. I have just agreed to end a person's life. I feel numb at the thought of this. How is it that my life has changed so much in a year? I used to dream of shopping sprees and sleepovers, and now I'm agreeing to kill a stranger.

The President's hologram flickers on. Her 3D image is so clear, it feels as if she is in the room with us.

"Condors, I want you to know how deeply grateful I am for your commitment to the Commonwealth of California. I know for many of you this is personal. It is for me as well. I've had seven family members taken by the Other 49, and I want nothing more than their freedom, along with the freedom of the thousands of others who are trapped in that camp. I need you to understand that Operation Tempest will make sure our nation remains a sovereign country free from the grip of tyranny and hate. Operation Tempest must be your focus. We have recently discovered an area in California bordering Arizona that has aqualinium. This makes getting those files to us even more important. As you enter the labor camp, you will see horrors beyond your imagination, but you need to stay clear-eyed on getting the files. Find the officer, get to the location, download the information, and get it back to us. Our future is in your hands. Understand?"

"Yes, Madam President," we say.

I don't really understand politics, but even I understand that if the Other 49 isn't the only country that has aqualinium, they stand to lose a lot of power and control over the rest of the world. If California has aqualinium, and we figure out how to use it, we will be able to control weather patterns too.

"How will we mine it?" I ask.

Everyone turns to me in surprise yet again. I always seem to ask questions at the wrong time. Or maybe I actually shouldn't be asking questions at all.

"This is becoming a regular thing with you, soldier," the President says. "May I ask *you* a question?" She chuckles and continues without waiting for my response. "Why did you become a Condor?"

"Ma'am?" I ask, totally confused.

"What is driving you to risk your life for the freedom of others?"

"My . . . my . . . mami," I say, blinking back my tears.

"Your mother is in the camp?"

"I think so."

"I am very sorry to hear that. I know how hard it is to have family members ripped away and forced into the camp. She's lucky to have you fighting for her."

I swallow hard. The lump in my throat feels like a lead ball.

I want to burst into tears, but I know I can't. I know for Mami's sake I must stay strong, hide my tears, and act as if none of this affects me. The President continues. "As you know, we're planning on exploding the mine. This will serve as a distraction for you to get inside, but at the same time, one thousand SOLIS soldiers will be raiding the camp. Their mission will be to free our family members, our friends, the soon-to-be citizens of California. Our soldiers will put them on trucks and bring them back to California. Any DF officers we capture will be our prisoners of war. And we will have them mine aqualinium for us in California."

I think about everyone who has been hurt by the DF. Every single person I know and all the people I don't know. I think about the girl at the border who was blown up by a land mine placed by a government who hated her so much they would do anything to keep her out. Her name was Solis. She was fifteen years old. We took her name as our own so no one would forget why we were fighting:

S—SVATANTRATA
O—OMINIRA
L—LIBERTAD
I—INKULULEKO
S—SELIPHAP

Each letter of her name stands for *liberty* in a different language: Hindi, Yoruba, Spanish, Zulu, and Loa. Liberty for us all. Liberty for those who have been hunted, disappeared, lied to, and killed.

But this plan of taking DF officers as prisoners of war and making them dig for aqualinium in California makes me ask myself, do we now get to do terrible things to our oppressors because they did unimaginable things to us? Isn't the race for aqualinium about preserving human life, not destroying it completely? I don't say any of this out loud, of course. I just keep thinking of Mami lighting her candles at the altar, asking for blessings and compassion for all beings. I don't know what she would say to this plan, but it's the only path forward as far as I can see. *Please, Mami*, I say in my head. *I just want to see you again. I just want you safe so we can all be together—you, me, and Ernie*. In order to get her back, I have to push all these questions and thoughts out of my mind. I must follow orders.

"This plan makes sense to me," I say to the President and everyone else in the room.

LILIANA

Querida Valentina,

There are hundreds of eyes on me at all times. The DF with their venomous gazes—even behind their masks, I can feel their hot glares. The cameras mounted to every cage, tent, or doorway. And then of course the eyes in the skies—their fleet of drones that swoop and zip around us at all times. Their constant buzz makes my head throb. I know they cannot see my thoughts, but sometimes at night I wake up in a cold sweat fearing they have found a way to read my mind.

For a few seconds in the dead of night, I think they have discovered Nelini's secret, our secret. I panic thinking it's my fault that SOLIS, our only hope for escape, has been discovered. Yes, I realize my fear is completely unfounded. I swear, I have not repeated a single word Nelini told me to anyone. But my sleep is always restless now. My mind wanders between the possible excitement of escape, the fear of getting caught, and the finality of death.

It's been four days since Nelini told me about SOLIS. I am ashamed to say I have not gone to the outhouse to see what she left for me. I am scared, mi'ja. I do not know if I can do what Nelini imagined I could. I am not sure I can bear the burden of this great responsibility.

Please, Vali, do not be disappointed in me or misunderstand my reasons for wanting to stay in this hellhole. I despise it here. I pray for freedom every day and fantasize about our miraculous reunion in California! I do!

But the thought of being in charge of leading everyone in here to freedom—it takes my breath away. How can this great plan of escape rest entirely on my shoulders? I worked at a farm. What do I know about resistance and revolutions? I know how to birth a cow. I know how to mother, how to make Ernie feel better when his belly hurts. I know how to braid your hair and talk to you about boys and sex and your period. I was not meant to be some grand hero or warrior.

The burden of Nelini's secret is almost too much to bear. I am having a hard time focusing on my work. Yesterday, I reached into a box to pull out another bag of stale grain and it broke in my hands. The grain spilled everywhere—in the box, on the floor, in my lap.

The DF officer who was watching yelled at me.

"Pick them up! Every last one of them."

He stood there as I crawled on my hands and knees, trying to gather up every single morsel. I was hoping he would get bored with this, but he kept pointing out pieces that I'd missed. Every time I picked up a piece of grain, I thought about Nelini. How disappointed she must be in me. Why did she choose me? I lost my best friend, and now I am ignoring her dying wish. I've been lying awake in our cage for what seems like hours. Little Isa is tucked into my arms fast asleep. She is such a sweet girl. She deserves so much more than these metal bunks and putrid food. Somehow this child smiles through this misery and loves me with abandon. I am grateful to her, but also I am so scared to be responsible for her. If I do as Nelini asked and get caught, what will become of little Isa?

I hear the sirens calling us to the morning roll call and harvest. My body sinks into the cold metal bed. It feels as if it weighs a million pounds. The harvests have been happening almost every morning now. I sit up slowly. Death rests on my shoulders.

The cage is dark except for the constant icy-blue lights radiating from everyone's wrists. In less than an hour, some wrists will flash, announcing their demise. An SOS to a God who most likely won't hear them. I stand up and start to make my way to the flagpole, our gathering spot for death. Every morning as I walk to the harvest, I pray I won't be chosen. Today, I don't even have the energy for that simple prayer. I am numb as I make my way there. I feel empty. I am devastated to say I do not even feel my love for you or Ernesto.

We shuffle into our lines, and thousands of us stand in silence. This has become our routine. The DF officers shout at us. We sing. The chips of those chosen for the harvest flash. And death comes for them. I don't even feel relief when my chip doesn't flash. But there is a scream so deafening, it rips right through me. I turn to see Rania on her knees, her arms wrapped around Kenna's waist. I am not sure which one of them has been chosen. I run toward the tragedy unfolding for all of us to witness. Rania wails with an agony so powerful it threatens to crack open the sky. Kenna gently caresses her face. She wipes Rania's tears with her long, slender hands. Oh, mi'ja, that's when I see it's Kenna's chip that is flashing. I cannot breathe. How is it that this child who has already lost so much is now losing her life and her love? I curse God at that moment!

Why have you abandoned us? How can you exist and allow this to happen to us? How can you just sit there and do nothing?

Kenna kneels in front of Rania. She looks her in the eyes, and I see her mouth the words I love you. *I want to look away. I am ashamed of being here. I hate that*

I am being forced to watch their pain as if they are a spectacle at a zoo.

I see a DF officer approaching. He's bashing through the lines of people, pushing feeble bodies out of his way. He is like a rabid dog, searching for prey. Without thinking, I stand in front of Rania and Kenna. I put my body between him and them. I want to give their love as much time to live as possible. Out of nowhere, a woman I have never spoken to before comes and stands next to me. Then another woman who sleeps in our cage stands on the other side of me. Before long, there is a circle of people standing shoulder to shoulder around Rania and Kenna. We are the barrier between life and death.

The officer is so close now, I can see his eyes. I take the women's hands in mine and plant my feet. The DF officer charges toward us at full speed. I brace myself for his impact. His shoulder slams into my chest. I hear the sound of my ribs cracking. I fall back, prepared to hit the ground, but something extraordinary happens. Hands, so many hands, catch me before I fall and place me back on my feet. I remain a barrier between the officer and Rania and Kenna. I stand tall and look into his eyes again. And for just an instant, he seems shocked, maybe even a bit afraid of me, of us.

Then, just as quickly, he snaps into action, pulling out his baton and beating us mercilessly. Bones crack under his lashes, heads smash to the ground. Our bodies are no match for his weapons and his hate. He breaks through our circle in seconds. He grabs Kenna by the neck and drags her away. Rania shrieks. She tries to run after Kenna, but I grab her and hold on to her as if she was you. I will not let her go. Rania will not die today too. She kicks, scratches, and punches me. She is so desperate to get to Kenna, but my grip on her is that of a mother; it is ironclad.

Now I can barely see what's happening because blood is gushing from a cut in my head. It gets into my eyes, and all I can see is a red blur. But I don't need to see to know what is going to happen. I hear the harvest cage locking and the screech of the pulley as it transports its victims over the mouth of the pit. Rania collapses onto the ground and pounds at the dirt over and over with her fists. The clank of the aqualinium canisters being loaded and the whoosh of their contents being launched into the sky silences us all.

Except for Rania. She curls up in a ball and wails Kenna's name again and again. She is like a baby lying there, so fragile and so alone.

The screams from the cage as the acid rain descends on them is horrific. But above the screams we hear Kenna's voice singing to us. She is sounding out these sacred chords that weave between this painful present and whatever we can dream for our future. Never once does Kenna scream from the pain that must be overwhelming her. I want to believe this was her last gift to Rania. It was an offering of kindness in her last moments on this Earth. She gave Rania the gift of having her beautiful song be the last thing she heard from her on that terrible morning.

I will not let Rania see the burnt and melted bodies as they are taken away. I make her look into my eyes as she repeats Kenna's name. I try to stop time for her, try to hold back the flood of pain that is drowning her. The women who formed the circle around Kenna and Rania approach us. The whispers of their condolences dance in the space between the living and the end, agony and love. Their hands gently touch Rania's arms, her back, her hair. Kenna's body is dragged out of the cage and thrown into a large wheelbarrow. I hear the hollow smack of her body hitting the metal. It feels like a blow to my heart. I look to where Kenna lies dying. I must bear witness to the end of this extraordinary life. I will hold the unbearable pain of Kenna's loss because that is all I can do now.

As she is being carted away, Kenna's arm tumbles out of the wheelbarrow. Her fingers drag along the dirt. I see they are moving. She is clinging to life. Slowly, three of her fingers curl into her palm, her thumb points out and her index finger extends. At first I do not know what she is doing, but then I see it. She has made the letter L. *This is her last message to us: liberty, freedom, liberation.*

Memories of Kenna as a young girl flash before my eyes. I see her eyes twinkle as she eats arepas with you on a Sunday morning. Remember how she loved my arepas? I hear her laughter as we teach her how to dance salsa in our kitchen. She spent countless evenings at our place doing homework. She was always so joyful and kind. She will forever be our family.

The DF officers hover around us. Their agitation is a warning that more violence will come if we do not end our mourning. The work in the mine stops for no one. Rania must continue to the mine, and I must go to the kitchen.

This harvest has changed me. By taking away Kenna, they have taken away my fear. Where I was numb before, I am now enraged. I do not want revenge; I want our freedom. And it is clear now there is only one path to freedom: SOLIS.

I am silent as I work in the kitchen. I chop rotting carrots and push the pieces of pale orange mush into a pot of boiling water. An officer walks by me and grunts in disgust at the food. And without thinking, I say, "Excuse me, sir. Can I go to the bathroom?"

Mi'ja, I feel Nelini pulling the words from my mouth.

"No. You're already behind."

"But, sir, I have a woman issue I need to take care of. My per—"

"Shut up! Just go. Get out of here." He swats at me with his baton and then walks away from me.

These men are stupid, mi'ja. You mention a period and they turn into man babies. Also, if they knew anything about our bodies, they would know no one in here is getting their periods. We are too malnourished to ovulate. We are little more than dust.

But they also don't know what we are capable of, clearly.

I run to the outhouse behind the second tent. There aren't any officers lurking about. I close the door behind me. It does not lock, so I say a prayer to God. Padre Nuestro, don't give me reason to curse you again.

The outhouse is made of small bricks. It has a tin roof and no electricity. The hole that Nelini was referring to is the hole where we do our "business." It is disgusting, and I will spare you the details except to tell you the brick Nelini spoke of is next to it. I kneel and instantly gag at the smell of shit and piss. I push down the sour bile as it rises up my throat. My body will not stop me from getting what's behind that brick.

As horrible as this is, I have to say Nelini was smart as hell. No one in their right mind would willingly come looking for anything here. Besides the harvest, this is the last place anyone wants to be. I reach past the hole and press the last brick, in the last row just as Nelini instructed. It is loose! I jiggle it, push it, and finally pull it out of its place. There is a paper folded just as Nelini promised there would be. Mi'ja, my hands shake wildly as I pull the paper out and replace the brick right away. I can't stop my hands from trembling. I am so scared and excited and baffled by all of this. The paper is crisp and clean resting in my palm. Nelini must have put it in there when she first started to get sick.

If you are reading this, I am already dead. What happens next is up to you.

SOLIS wants to help us escape, but they can't do it alone. They need us to help them from the inside.

There are four things you must do to escape.

Get matches.

Find a way for methane to accumulate in the mine.

Collect as much aqualinium as you can; it's an explosive when mixed with methane and fire.

Use the aqualinium, methane, and match to set off an explosion in the mine.

Tell SOLIS when the plan is ready. When a drone falls from the sky, that means they're ready to help you escape, and then you can detonate the explosive.

If you think you will be chosen for the harvest, find someone to replace you. Do not let your death be the death of everyone.

I have so many questions that no one can give me answers to. This paper is all I have. Cryptic instructions that might get me killed but also might give us our freedom. I have no choice but to trust Nelini and trust myself. This is always the hardest part of faith for me. I was raised to believe in our Holy Father, the all-merciful protector and provider. But believing in myself . . . this is a new and terrifying task.

I must try. I cannot ignore this call to arms, though I have no idea how I can possibly get it done. This plan feels so hopeful and hopeless all at once. How can I possibly do this without being caught? And who exactly will be waiting on the other side of the walls?

I read Nelini's message over and over until I memorize it. Besides the actual plan, if I can even call it that, she left me instructions for how to communicate with SOLIS on the back side of her note. I will write tomorrow and tell them about Nelini. Once I do this, there's no going back. I'll be leading the mission. I put the note in its place behind the brick. I pray I do not need to pass this plan on to anyone else. I believe I can do it. I smile to myself. Nelini was una loca, and I will love her until the end of my days.

For the first time since I got here, I feel possibility igniting my every move. I even have to bite my lip to keep from smiling. I must admit, I do love imagining the mine exploding into a fiery madness.

I think you will be impressed with me, mi'ja. I think you will be proud.

I am ready to fight.

JESS

After our morning roll call, I stumble my way back to the medical tent.

Of course, I know there is nothing remotely medical or healing about this tent and the DF officer in charge here is certainly no doctor. Like most of the things I was told by the DF and chose to believe, this is all a pack of lies. From what I heard whispered in the cage last night, it sounds like this tent is for performing depraved experiments on any prisoners who've been exposed to the artificial rains. If they survive, their consolation prize is a trip to this special place, where the DF gets as many samples of their blood and tissues as possible before they die. Then the New American Republic can study all those pieces of broken people and perfect their formula to make the water drinkable.

Essentially, everyone here is a human guinea pig. And I have been given the "honor" of being the mad scientist's assistant. I cannot think of a crueler punishment. The moment I step into this tent again, I'm breathless. The wails and whimpers, sobs and smells, are all around me.

"Help, please!" I hear someone cry from one of the beds.

"Mama," another begs.

These are human beings! I want to yell.

Yes, it has taken me too long to learn this truth. And yes, I realize that my outrage helps exactly no one. But what else can I do? I have hurt everyone in this tent, in this camp, in this soulless country. Maybe I didn't erect the tents, but I cheered when people were rounded up and brought here. I signed up for the DF and boasted about wanting to make my first capture. I memorized the anthem and pulled the trigger in the desert. I am part of the reason this exists, and I hate myself for it now.

"Start with the buckets!" orders the officer in charge.

I'm moving much slower today. Even with Liliana's help, I'm still stiff and sore along my ribs and back. My ears are ringing, and there is a gash by my eye that continues to ooze.

"What are you doing?" asks one of the patients. "Get back in bed before she sees you!"

"No, I'm one of . . ." I don't know what to say. I'm one of them? I'm one of you? "They told me to empty the buckets," I offer. It's not an explanation, but it's all I know for sure.

For the rest of the morning, I try to look at each person lying here as I take the buckets in and out. Each face seems to have a million things to say. Each moan could be their last message.

The officer in charge here storms in at some point and demands I hurry up.

"I was working on the waste buckets," I tell her.

"You want a medal or a monument? Wheel in the next one."

I try to give the next patient a smile as I bring her into the room and strap her onto the operating table. She is barely conscious, which I count as a blessing. Her body is covered in scabs and seeping wounds; her eyes are lost in a tormented fog.

I wish I could just wheel her in and then leave, but I think the officer likes that I have to watch her mutilate these victims. Plus, selfishly, I can't help thinking about the needle and thread that Liliana asked me to retrieve for her. I find it so strange that she wants to stitch me back together. More than that, Liliana is the first person who's cared for me in I don't know how long.

"Forceps!" the officer shouts at me.

I do as I'm told. While I have an excuse to be by the supply cabinet, I also scan the shelves, looking for a needle and thread. Of course, all I see in this tent are little jars full of specimens and dirty syringes. There's no needle and thread or even bandages in sight—which makes sense. It's not as if the DF is in the business of helping people feel better. The patient on the table is definitely awake now, jerking her body and begging for this barbaric procedure to end.

"Where are my forceps?!" the officer bellows. I have it in my hand, but I still have to find the needle and thread for Liliana. I'm opening and closing drawers now, the officer getting louder and angrier by the second. "What the fuck?!"

All I find is a knot of bloody string and some sort of blade with a hole in it. I don't know how they'll work, but I hide them both in my sleeve as quickly as possible and turn back to the officer. She grabs the forceps and slaps me across the face.

"Fucking useless!" she roars, returning to her victim with even more gusto.

The patient is now flailing and shrieking. I can't look, but I also can't turn away. She is a mess of skin and bones and desperation. There's blood and entrails everywhere. She doesn't want to die. Not like this. Please not like this.

I step toward her just as she seizes and then goes still.

"Look what you made me do!" the officer snarls at me. I don't know how me handing her the forceps either helped or hurt the situation. But the officer is livid. She kicks the operating table with her steel-toed boot and tosses her forceps at my head, just narrowly missing my swollen eye.

"Throw her in the pit!" she says. "And don't come back! You're going to the mine from now on!"

I don't know how to breathe. I don't know how to push this now-dead being outside to her open grave. But somehow I do. I follow orders. I get that woman who was alive just a few minutes ago and cart her away. I hoist her off the gurney and place her onto a growing pile of corpses as gently as possible. Then I crouch next to her, gasping, trying to make sense of what just happened.

I don't know why I'm not in that pit myself. I put my hand on the dead woman's shoulder. I feel her bones beneath her burlap sack—the outline of how she once lived. She could've been a dancer or a scientist, a hairdresser or a race car driver. She was someone's mother or sister, cousin or wife. And now she's another sacrifice to this carnage.

I don't know what to do with myself. I cower behind the medical tent. I'm sure some drone or maniac officer will come and beat me senseless soon enough. Let them take me. Let them hack me open and pull out whatever is left of my heart. Eventually, I hear the siren announcing the evening roll call. Still, I just stay there, wondering how anyone can tell time in a place like this. Time doesn't make sense. Nothing does.

Nothing except the moaning.

At first, I think it's coming from one of the patients inside. But all the tent's openings are sealed shut. I think the officer in charge has left for the day. So have all of her DF helpers. There's nobody else alive out here. Or at least that's what I thought.

There's more than moaning now. It's the most agonizing sound—like someone is gasping for air and drowning at the same time. I look around, trying to figure out where the noise is coming from. I circle the medical tent again. And again. I think part of me knows what's going on, but I can't imagine it being true, until I lean down over that pit of dead bodies. I hear the noise much more clearly now, which can only mean . . .

There is someone in the pit who is still alive.

My breath is coming so fast now. How do I possibly find this person? I try to ease a shoulder up, and roll a body to the side, uncovering another. And another. Each time I see another lifeless figure, I want to shake it, hold it, cry for it. But there is still someone making noise. There is someone who needs my help. As my eyes travel over this mess of limbs and jaws, hair and teeth, I see a blood-speckled hand move ever so slightly. It looks like it's trying to grasp on to something . . . Air? Life?

There is someone pinned down under at least three other bodies, desperately trying to wriggle free. They must hear me panting, because they say, "Pleeeeease."

"Are you okay?" I whisper. The stupidest question to ask.

"Pleeeeease," she tries again. Her voice is so thin and high when she tries to make words. I don't want her to make any more words. I don't want her to be struggling for air like this.

"Can I do something?" I ask. "Can I . . . ?"

"Pleeeuuuuh—" she says, her hand scooping desperately at the air. I want to run away so fast and so far. But I can't. I have to go into the pit. I crawl inside, feeling the flesh and bones squish and crack under me. I roll body after body away. The groaning is getting louder and louder as I do.

There she is. Gulping in air and soaked in blood. It's dim out now, but I can make out her hands, her lips, her forehead.

"Pleeaaa—" she tries.

I don't know what to do. This body is struggling so mightily.

No, not this body. This *person*. This person who is trying to say something between staggered breaths. Most of her face is covered in blisters and blood; her chin pokes out, quivering. I reach out to wipe away some of the blood, and she jolts. Her eyes look wild, darting around trying to make sense of what she sees. Trying to blink this moment into focus.

That's when I realize who this is. It's that girl with the ebony skin and blazing stare. She's the one I saw holding hands with Rania. She's the one who made those kids laugh and sing, who looked like she'd actually found some kind of joy and even love before they destroyed her in the harvest.

Kenna. That was her name when she was full of life.

Now she is lying among the dead, moments away from death herself. There is no way I can get her out of this pit without breaking her more.

"It's okay . . . ?" I try to sound soothing, but it comes out more like a plea of my own.

Every breath seems to wrack Kenna's body and bring tears to her wandering eyes. She swipes at the air again, and I can't take it. I reach out. As my fingers touch hers, she latches on and squeezes.

Her skin is wet and cold. She starts thrashing and chattering, gripping my fingers tightly.

"It's gonna be okay," I say. Again and again.

So what if I'm feeding her lies? So what if I can't stop the blood or the shaking? At least I stay. I stay and hold Kenna's hand as she suffers unbearably. I can't tell if I'm with her for minutes or hours. Soon, there is just a sliver of light falling on the ground.

"Shhh," I say over and over, humming just like Liliana did for me after Nick and his friends beat me to a pulp.

Kenna's breathing starts getting slower, stuttering and then disappearing for longer and longer pauses.

As her grip on me loosens, I stroke her hand. She has that little twisted shoelace wrapped around her wrist that is dripping with blood, and underneath it, I find her pulse, fading, fading.

Until she exhales, then exhales again, sinking down with a quiet creak.

And I know she is gone.

"It's okay," I say one last time. I don't know who I'm talking to anymore. But I do know that I've finally done something kind for someone else. And before letting Kenna's lifeless hand go, I pull off that bloody shoelace from her wrist and hold it in a tight fist. Then I carry it back to our cage.

So I can give it to Rania and tell her there was peace at the end.

RANIA

After they carry Kenna away to the "medical" tent . . .

After I shriek and wail and claw at everyone and everything in this heartless universe . . .

After I work all day in that pit filled with deadly fumes and scores of people who are almost dead too . . .

I come back to the cage, to the pallet where I once held Mama, and then held Kenna, and now hold . . .

Nothing.

The world becomes just this hole that I have to crawl through. No, it's a tunnel. It's one of those pipes under the outhouses, full of feces and gurgling green horrors. And I have to get through it because I know Kenna is in here somewhere, somehow. She *has* to be.

"Kenna!" I call out. "Kenna, I'm coming!"

The sewage is getting higher and higher, and sometimes my head slips under, my mouth and nose filling with disgustingness. I scrape at the walls all around me, but I can't go fast enough. Everything is closing in on me. I have to clear through all the stinking refuse between me and her. And while part of me knows that it's impossible, another part will not let me quit.

"Kenna!" I warble through the muck.

I need to touch her skin. I need to find her sparkling eyes. Is that her voice I hear in the distance? I need her to tell me where she is so I can get us both out of here. I splash and flail, scooping out a passageway only to have it fill up again.

"Kenna! It's me! Please just tell me where you are!"

I swear, I will carry her on my back as I crawl through here. Or I'll bind her to my chest and swim my way through. I don't care if there are DF officers on the other side of the walls. I would stand in front of an entire squadron of vengeful officers if I could just hold Kenna again.

"Pleeeeaaaase!" I scream.

"*Rania.*" I hear a voice coming from somewhere beyond these pipes. Then I feel a hand squeezing my shoulder, shaking me gently. "Rania, *breathe*."

Could it be that Kenna's already made it to the other side? I find the hand and grip it tight, pulling her into me.

"Wake up," says the voice.

When I open my eyes, it's not Kenna I'm clutching. It's Liliana. Her face is practically touching mine, and I can see the capillaries in her eyeballs spreading out in lacy webs. Her cheeks are damp; I think she's been crying. She squeezes my shoulder again and wipes my forehead with her warm palm.

"Rania, you have to breathe. Please."

"No!" I don't mean to yell at her. I know she means well, but this is not how it was supposed to go. "Where is she?" I screech. "Where is Kenna?!"

Liliana winces but stays firm.

"Please, just breathe."

I look around me, the cage refusing to come into focus. Everything is so blotchy and jumbled.

"Look. I have some broth for you," Liliana offers, lifting a cup to my lips. I don't want any of it. I don't want to taste or touch anything until I know that Kenna is here. But Liliana will not give up. "Rania, listen. We will walk through this together. We will find a way. And Jess has brought you something . . ."

Then the white girl moves into my line of vision. She is still bruised and scarred, but there's something strangely serene about her as she steps toward me. Maybe even confident. She opens her palm and shoves it in my face.

"I thought you'd want this," she says. Is she grinning?

I look down and see she's handing me a blood-soaked shoelace tied in a small loop with a frayed knot barely holding it together.

"What is that?" I say. "Why are you giving this to me?" I don't know what this girl wants, but there's no place for her in my brain right now.

"It was on her wrist . . . ?" the white girl says tentatively. She holds it next to the matching shoelace on my wrist, then pauses, waiting for me to catch up. "Your . . . girlfriend?"

A wave of nausea and desperation rocks my whole being.

It feels like everything inside me is splintering open and there's no way to put any of my pieces back together. I just stare at the white girl. I know what she's *trying* to say—that this is Kenna's bracelet. And Kenna is gone. But that cannot be true. I will not *let* that be true.

I'm the one who was supposed to bring Kenna to freedom. *I'm* the one who was going to go with her through the tunnels or scale the walls—whatever it took—to get out of here. *I'm* the one Kenna loved and wanted by her side now and forever. We were going to get a bungalow and plant a lemon tree together. Maybe we'd get a secondhand piano and I'd play soft classical music while Kenna sang and then we would kiss in the grocery store and read stories to each other at night. We had it all worked out. We were almost ready to go!

The white girl doesn't know what to make of my silence. She looks at Liliana and asks whether she should just leave the bracelet there or maybe save it for another time. Liliana thanks her and tries to talk to me again. But her words are ridiculous and cruel.

"Rania. Listen to me. Kenna is gone. She passed away. I'm so very sorry. But Jess was in the medical tent with her. She held Kenna's hand until she took her last breath. And she brought you—"

"No! No, no, no, no!"

I'm so breathless with rage. I howl with as much fury as I can muster. My throat is raw and ragged from screaming. Still, the white girl just stands there, gaping at me like I'm some exotic beast. I hate her so much—her shell-shocked stare, her quivering lip. I want to slice her open and make her feel real pain.

"What do you want?!" I grab the bracelet from her and fling it in her face. "You want me to *thank* you? To *applaud* you? This is all your fault! *You* killed her! You *killed* the only person I had left!"

I lunge at her ashen face, trying to dig my broken fingernails into her skin. She has no idea what I'm capable of! I will tear her flesh from bone and pull out her still-beating heart if that's what it takes!

Liliana is too fast, though. She wraps her sturdy arms around my middle and pries me away as I thrash and swipe at the air. Then she brings me over to her little sleeping area and tries to calm me down. She holds me tight and whispers into my hair, "I know, this is so hard. I know."

How can she *know*?

She can't!

She can't know how every bone in my body is breaking, how every memory or dream I think of is being snuffed out and I have nobody to blame except myself.

Kenna! I didn't know they were going to call you up to the harvest! I was stupid and scared, and I would climb through a thousand pipes if you could just come back now!

I think of when Baba was taken. And when Mama told me to run. I picture those days of scrabbling and scrambling through back alleys to get away from the DF, sucking on pebbles or scrub brush for some kind of nourishment. But none of that is as sharp and all-encompassing as this agony.

"It's all my fault," I tell Liliana. I can't hold on to all this guilt and grief any longer. "She had a plan to get us out of here and I told her I wasn't ready. *Wasn't ready?!*"

"Shhh," Liliana says, pulling me into her chest. "This is not your fault."

"Yes, it is! It's my fault they chose her!"

I cannot stop replaying last night in my mind. Kenna's head on my shoulder, her long fingers interlaced with mine. Her dreams of eating mangoes and the way her kisses made me quiver.

"This is not fair," Liliana says. "And it is not your fault."

I do not know what happens after this. I do not want to know. I stay there, sobbing in Liliana's arms for hours, just letting myself dissolve. I hear Isa and Esteban singing their ABC song because that's what we usually do at this time of night. And as usual, Esteban says, "Ell mellow pee," instead of "L, M, N, O, P," which always made Kenna laugh.

But I don't laugh.

I don't join in.

Because I have nothing left to give.

JESS

I don't know why I ever thought handing Rania a bloody shoelace would make things better. At the same time, I wasn't expecting her to be so angry. I guess I didn't think any of this through.

"Can I just say . . . sorry? I didn't mean to make it worse. I was just trying to . . ."

Nobody's listening to me. The women are too busy crowding around Rania in a huddle, protecting her. I want to tell them that I was born into this fucked-up country and I thought I was defending some ideal. That I was breastfed this red, white, and blue bullshit and I thought it was the only way.

But even that's too much of a cop-out. It's *me*. I'm the one who signed up for the DF. I'm the one who pulled the trigger in the desert. I'm the one who memorized the anthem and truly believed I was part of some superior race. I did all of it.

The circle around Rania only gets tighter. Their voices are

soft and mournful, like a rumbling tide rolling in. There are whispers and weeping.

"I'm sorry," I say again. This time a little louder. Loud enough for a pair of eyes to turn around and peer out from the circle at me. It's one of the girls Rania's been teaching at night. She breaks apart from the other women and steps toward me, tugging on one of her frizzy braids. Her lips are pressed together in a short angry line.

"What do you want?" the girl demands. She comes up to about my belly button, but I'm kind of terrified. And she asks a fair question, even if I have no answer for her. I mean, what *do* I want? I want this whole thing to be over. I want to go back in time and tell Walter Winnecut in the desert to run before I shoot. No, I want to never have that gun in the first place. I want to tell Mom it's not *their* fault you don't have a job! You really think that some guy who brought his family to this country under the floorboards of a van so he could clean toilets at the local Wendy's is a *threat to America*? You think pouring acid rain on people is going to make our lives better?

"Hello?" the braided girl says. I can tell she is getting fed up with me just staring at her. But I'm not sure what to say.

"Never mind," I mumble. "It's not a good time."

"No, it's not," the girl moans. "I don't think it's ever going to be a good time again." Her eyes well up with tears. She starts sniffling and chews on her chapped, flaky lips. Great. Now I made the one person who'll talk to me cry.

"I know this must be hard on you too," I offer. "That girl who died—"

"Señorita Kenna," the girl cuts in. "They killed her with the experiment. They did that to my mommy too."

Her bravery floors me. "I'm so sorry," I whisper again. But what do those words even mean at this point?

The girl shrugs and kicks at the dirt floor. There is so much quivering under her skin, though. I can tell she is fighting back tears. I just want to hug her. I squat down so we can be eye to eye.

"It's not fair!" the girl wails. "Why do they keep pouring that stuff from the sky?"

"I don't know," I admit.

"It was just a little cough, but next maybe it'll be Señorita Rania or Liliana because anyone I like gets put in the harvest. And then I'll have nobody left at aaaaall!"

She is stomping her feet and chewing her lips so hard now that they're bleeding, and I have no answers for her. I have nothing to offer except myself. I open my arms to her. She sizes me up and then dives in, sobbing and wiping her nose on my disgusting sack. Her body is so tiny. I feel her bones poking through her skin. And then the most glorious thing happens. She hugs *me.* Her two little arms wrap around my waist, and it is the most beautiful thing I have experienced in what feels like forever.

It lasts for maybe all of five seconds, though. As soon as the evening sirens sound, the girl pulls away. She looks at me with a smile. I smile back.

"I have to get ready for escuela," she says. Then she scurries away, rejoining the group around Rania. I want to call her back, but I too have to get going. I was told as soon as I returned to the cage that I'd be starting my new night shift in the mine tonight. I'm actually due at the flagpole in a few minutes.

Just as I'm about to leave, though, Liliana comes toward me and murmurs, "You get the needle and thread?"

"Oh, yes! Or . . . something like that." I take out the little blade with the hole in it and the clump of bloody string from my sleeve where I hid it and hand the mess to her.

She looks at the supplies, then at my swollen eye.

"Do you want me to sew you now?" she asks.

"That's okay," I tell her. "I'm . . . fine." I don't know what she could do with that blade and string, and I don't want her to spend any more time trying to make me feel better. But before she turns away, I have to get out one more thing.

"I just want to say . . . thank you."

"It's okay."

The last siren for the night-shift workers is sounding. I don't know why I'm still standing here or what I can possibly add, but I look Liliana in the eyes and say, "I know I did horrible things. I know I'm an awful person. And I want to change that. I want to . . ."

Liliana breathes in as if she's about to say something, then swallows whatever words she had. I hope she heard me. I hope she understands.

"I'm serious," I tell her. "I mean, if I can help make this better in any way . . ."

She doesn't say a word. Just nods and walks away, calling the others to prayer.

LILIANA

Mi'ja, I think you'd be proud of me. I am fueled by my faith and ready to fight. Once I hear the drones circle past our tent tonight, I will pull out a slip of cardboard that I hid in my shoe from the kitchen. I will write my note to SOLIS on this cardboard. I will tell them I am their contact now. I am the leader. I will do whatever needs to be done for my people to be liberated.

Nelini organized this all so incredibly well. She left me detailed instructions on how to send and receive messages from SOLIS. She thought out every single step. I think of her whenever I have doubts. Her courage gives me courage.

I will write this note with the small vial of baking soda and water Nelini left me. I will watch it dry and disappear. And then tomorrow I will place it in the garbage heap. There are mounds and mounds of garbage bags being picked up tomorrow, and I have to place my note in one, then tie the top with an extra loop. This is our signal for the truck driver. He will deliver my message to SOLIS.

Once the letter is delivered to SOLIS, I only have fourteen days to get everything in order for our escape. My stomach ties itself in knots whenever I think about it, which is all the time. Three hundred and thirty-six hours doesn't feel like enough time to make the impossible possible. Twenty thousand one hundred and sixty minutes to figure out how to make methane accumulate in the mine (no clue how to do that) and gather enough aqualinium to make it explode (how do I get aqualinium out of the mine?), with a match to ignite the explosion (I hope I can steal matches from the kitchen).

This plan, as impossible as it is, fills me with hope and possibility. I do not know what to do with these emotions, as they feel almost foreign to me now. I am accustomed to dread and pain, not optimism and promise. These feelings don't seem to belong here inside of these walls. But they are alive and growing inside of me. I want to share them with Rania. She is so broken and in need of anything besides the grief that is consuming her.

For days I have watched as Rania comes up from the mine and sips her broth. She looks like a ghost; even her eyes are hollow. After the evening roll call she goes straight to the cages and crumples onto her pallet. She refuses to tell stories to little Isa and Esteban. She refuses everything and does nothing.

I try whispering in her ear, rubbing her back. She does not respond. The fog of her heartache is so thick. I don't know what else I can offer to make her talk to me again, to make her believe in all of these slips of possibility. Still, I have to try.

I decide to sing to her in honor of Kenna's memory. I think my song can draw her back from the abyss. It's the same song I sang to you when you were just a baby, a song passed down from my own mother. My voice is not beautiful. It cracks and squeaks off-key, but it carries a tenderness that Rania desperately needs.

"Rania, Rania, Rania, cierra los ojitos y verá que calma."

I sing softly, my words hanging in the air like a prayer. Still, there is no response. Her physical presence is here with us, but her soul, mi'ja, seems to have departed to another realm. She is not on this plane.

We sit in silence for a little while. I listen to the drones above us. The scattered coughs. This is our life right now. Not forever, but for right now. This is what I have to make Rania understand. I must bring her back to me so that together we can plot our escape. I want to tell her she will be free soon. In her newfound freedom, she'll be able to remember the echoes of Kenna's kiss, the warmth of her touch, and the whisper of her laughter. It won't be fair or enough, but at least this love story will be hers. I want to be able to give Rania this gift, but before I can, there are problems I need to figure out.

I wish I could ask Rania what she knows about methane gas in the mine and how we can sneak aqualinium out, but she can't give me answers right now. All I can do is keep singing. I notice the smallest sigh. Might this be an opening? A connection back to us?

"Rania, do you want something to eat? I have a fresh piece of bread I brought just for you."

Silence.

"You will not believe what I had to do to get the bread." I chuckle to myself hoping she will react to something.

"They normally keep the officers' pantry locked, but today the door didn't close all the way. I noticed immediately. I prayed to God no one else would see it. He answered my prayers, and at the end of my shift, I was able to get inside without anyone seeing me. Imagine, I was in there all by myself and I was completely surrounded by food! So much good food! I ate a bunch of bread, chips, and even chocolate! I grabbed what I could. I put pieces of bread up my sleeves, making sure it wasn't obvious. On the way out, I put a crumpled piece of paper in the lock. Hopefully

that will stop it from locking automatically. I was very scared. But I'm happy to have this bread to give to you. So please take it. It's delicious."

I place the bread in front of her. She doesn't move, but she doesn't reject it, which is a good sign. Maybe my voice will be her lifeline back to us. I keep talking, hoping that with each word she's one step closer to me.

"I had this idea for the kids. I was thinking maybe we should do something nice for Isa, Mishi, and Esteban. Vali and Ernie loved to put on fashion shows when they were little. They would walk down the runway pretending to wear all these special clothes. I would pretend I was the announcer, and describe their fancy outfits. It was so much fun. We played for hours! The outfits got crazier and crazier the longer we played. What do you think? Will they like it?"

Another sigh. I take that as a sign to keep going.

"I miss Vali and Ernesto so much it hurts my body. I think my dreams are the hardest part of all of this. I get to see them at night and then they're gone again in the morning. Last night, I dreamt Ernie was climbing inside the Statue of Liberty, up to the crown. You know you used to be able to do that? Climb hundreds of steps right on up! Imagine. Anyway, in my dream he kept begging me to climb the steps so we could see the ships come in through the windows in her crown. I kept saying no because I was scared. I don't know what I was

scared of; I was just scared. You know how we're always just scared here. It was like that feeling. But Ernesto didn't understand that fear. He wanted to go up the stairs—typical Ernesto. I begged him not to. I tried to stop him. I tried to follow him, but suddenly everything became dark. I couldn't see him anymore. So I just ended up in the staircase alone."

Silence.

"As hard as they are, I'd rather have the dreams than not." My voice cracks full of longing for my babies.

Rania rolls toward me and curls up again with a deep sigh. I'm not sure what she's thinking, and I definitely don't know what I should do next. I reach out to comfort her, half expecting her to push my hand away. But she stays lying there, motionless. As I move her hair out of her face, I see the skin surrounding her ear is raw and oozing from the toxic minerals in the mine. I want to give her a balm of some kind. I want to be *a balm for her, to soothe her deep pain. She has lost so much.*

I do not say anything more. What is there to say when the worst has already happened? Instead, I run my fingers through her hair. I feel her body unclench. Her eyes close, and her breathing quietly flutters in and out. Soon she is asleep the way you used to sleep on my lap. It feels good to mother her.

That's when I notice that every time I stroke Rania's

hair, little green specks shimmer on my skin. At first, I am confused. How did glitter end up in her hair? But then I realize it's aqualinium! I've never seen it before. I've only heard people talk about how it glows green inside the mine. When they extract it with their hands, the green dust covers their entire bodies. This glittering green shimmer is what coated Nelini's lungs, Kenna's lungs, and is in the process of invading Rania.

I look at Rania's sack that clings to her sleeping body. There are tiny green fragments nestled into the cloth. I'm amazed I've never noticed it before. It's easy to miss since the pieces of aqualinium are so tiny, yet it's so evident. This makes me wonder what other obvious things I'm overlooking here. What else has my pain and sadness made me blind to?

I realize that I need to change the way I am looking at this camp. I need to reframe what this camp is to me and to our mission. Instead of seeing it as a place keeping me away from you and Ernesto, I need to see it as the key to my escape. Everything I require to escape is here within these electrified walls. I only need to find it.

I fall asleep that night thinking of all the possibilities this camp holds. In my dreams I see tents being used as parachutes, metal pallets as ladders, drones as flying carpets. I wake up ready to unlock the secrets this place has been keeping from me.

After the morning roll call, I stir the officers'

breakfast mush. I look at the pot and ask myself, Can it help us get out? Can this ladle make methane accumulate? *The answer is NO! NO! And NO! But at some point there will be a yes. I just have to keep asking the questions. I recalibrate. I think it's best to start with what's easiest: the matches. I am in a kitchen; there must be matches in this place. An officer walks by smelling of cigarette smoke and sour body odor. Of course—he must have a match! All these stupid officers smoke. They all must have matches and lighters.*

I keep my eyes on him all day, hoping I can snatch his lighter. He is a literal chimney. I can't even count the amount of times he pulls out a lighter and starts puffing on a new cigarette. But there is no way I can steal his lighter without him realizing it's gone. It's practically tied to his fingers, taunting me the entire day. I am so mad. I am sure I'm going to fail. I can't even get a damn lighter or a match!

My stomach growls. I have not eaten all day. I've been focused on the officer and his cigarettes. I eye the officers' pantry. I wonder if that little paper has kept the door unlocked. When no one is looking, I push the handle down, and it unlocks!

¡Gracias, Dios mío santísimo!

Inside the pantry are stacks and stacks of food that rise to the ceiling. They never let the kitchen staff in here. The officers bring out the food we cook for them for every meal. They've kept this room their little secret. If people knew there was enough food in here to feed us for days, they might riot. At times, hunger can override fear.

I have to move quickly. I grab some bread and put it up my sleeve. I grab beef jerky and roll my sleeve over it to hide it. I scan the shelves, looking for food that is both nutritious and easy to sneak out of here. Then my eyes spot a box of cigarettes. If their cigarettes are stored in here, then maybe there are lighters too! My eyes desperately skim the shelves. I move boxes around but am careful to put everything back in its place. I am frantic and meticulous all at once. And then, finally, in the back of the fourth row, I find a box of lighters. My heart dances in my chest as my fingers slide through the plastic film and grab our fiery hope. I take the jerky out of my sleeve and replace it with the lighter. I open the door and slip out of the pantry without anyone seeing.

At nightfall, I get back to our cage and collapse. The room is quiet and mostly empty. People are eating or sleeping or slowly dying in their corners. I am so full of fear and faith. I unroll my sleeve and slide out the lighter. There is a small space between the bunk beds and the dirt. I uncover the hole where the little blade and string are and pull them out from under the bed. After so much time in this prison, I have learned to never throw anything away. Our lives are so precarious, and we have so little, that anything can become a lifeline. I stare at the little blade in my hand. I wonder how it can help get us out of here. It is small, almost insignificant, but along with the lighter, it is a tool I must use for our freedom. Suddenly, I see its purpose.

I thread the string through the blade's hole so it can act as a needle. Then I flip up the bottom part of my burlap sack and start to sew a hem. It's not easy. The blade isn't as nimble as a needle, but it will do. Just as I had hoped, a hemmed burlap sack looks exactly like one that isn't. I fall back in bed, laughing at the madness of this all. The hem of this burlap dress will be the key to our liberation. Mi'ja, this is how we will get the aqualinium out of the mine and hide it! My only task is to get my hands on an extra burlap dress. This will be difficult, but it is not out of the question.

Because this whole plan is crazy but not impossible. It is terrifying, but maybe attainable. I don't have the answers, but I am willing to risk everything for the dream that it will lead me back to you, mi'ja.

And now I must take the biggest risk of all and tell others about the plan. There are things I simply cannot do—like gathering aqualinium from the mine.

I take advantage of the relative quiet of our cage and think through exactly who might be willing to help me. The two women who stood next to me as I tried to protect Kenna are clearly brave and have some sort of rebellious streak in them. I can ask them. And maybe Jess, la gringa, can help too. She gave Isa her breakfast the other day. Her kindness surprised me. Maybe she'd be willing to put herself at risk. She has nothing to lose now. I wish I could ask Rania to join in, but I know she is too lost in her grief right now. So I will have to start with those three. I'll put hems in their burlap sacks, and I'll have them sneak out penny-sized pieces of aqualinium.

Vali, it will be terribly hard to ask these women to sign on to this plan. It is a big ask. If they get caught, they could be brutally punished. Even if they don't get caught, the mineral is harsh and makes people's skin raw and blistered. I'm asking them to expose themselves to it for longer. I'm asking them to keep it by their skin, to inhale the dust, to run toward the aqualinium instead of away from it. I've never worked in the mine. I don't know what it is truly like down there. So I can't blame them for doubting me or turning away. But I'll ask anyway.

I have faith in people. And soon we will fill a dress with aqualinium, and it will be our radiant resistance.

RANIA

I have no idea how I'm alive when Kenna is gone, how I can feel hunger and thirst when her body is rotting in a pit. The planet spinning on some axis while hurtling through space makes no sense to me. I sift through these images of my past and wonder: *Why am I still here? How does my heart keep pumping blood, how do my lungs keep breathing in and out, when I'm drowning in bottomless grief?* It's an ache so deep and intense, it smothers me. This is the real punishment—harsher than anything the DF can design or manufacture—keeping me alive so I have to feel it all.

I don't even have the energy to talk to the kids. They don't need me anyway. Isa and Esteban know what they're doing by now. They help Mishi to sound out her letters and numbers. Meanwhile, I tally up the number of days, hours, and minutes that I've somehow continued without Kenna.

So far it's been seven days, fourteen hours, and somewhere around thirty minutes. They confiscated all our watches, of course. I just can't help hearing the sirens and trying to chart time, to quantify this grief that feels unending.

The warning siren for the night-shift crew sounds; a few women have to leave for the mine—including the white girl. It's kind of funny to think of her having to get lowered into that cavernous pit and dig for aqualinium. I heard they won't even give her a pickaxe or hammer, which makes digging even more brutal on the body. Her hands are stripped raw and shaking every time I see her.

Including right now, as she squeezes Liliana's hand and nods before adjusting her headlamp and walking toward the officer waiting at our cage door.

Is Liliana friends with her now? What was that nod and hand squeeze about?

Before I can ask, though, Liliana circles everyone up for prayers.

"Come on, Rania, please?" she asks. She does this every night, even though I've made it clear that I'd rather roll myself into the musty blanket full of memories and squeeze my eyes shut until someone makes me get up again.

I listen to her gathering everyone together, asking for some divine intervention.

"Ángel de Dios, mi querido guardián, me presento hoy ante ti para agradecerte y pedirte que siempre estés a mi lado, para que guíes, ilumines y gobiernes mi vida."

Liliana's voice is hoarse but steady. Other people join in too, picking up a phrase here or there like loose threads. There's nothing holding the words together. No reason to believe any of this can help. Maybe Mama would be proud of me now—finally embracing silence.

Liliana starts naming the dead, the missing, the sick. These lists are getting so long, I shut my eyes to block them out. Only, as I'm about to, I see a small stooped woman making her way toward Liliana. The woman's eyes are ringed in dark circles of fear, and her arms are spotted with boils.

"Please!" she rasps. "I have a name to add!" She lifts a trembling fist and puts it in Liliana's open palm. "Elian Sallah," the woman says. She looks at Liliana long and hard and then releases her fist and walks away.

"I have a name too," says another woman who's never spoken at our circle before. She hobbles over and does the same thing—adding a brief prayer while holding Liliana's hand, then letting go and retreating. This goes on for a while, women walking over to Liliana, taking her hand in theirs, and saying a few words. Often with a pointed look at Liliana too, sometimes a nod. This is not the way Liliana's prayer circle usually goes. Usually, maybe a dozen people stand up in a circle; the rest chime in from their sleeping pallets or just listen.

There's something that feels very different about this whole thing. Meanwhile, Liliana doesn't seem disturbed or curious about any of it. Instead, she keeps squeezing everyone's hands and nodding. Adding a smile here and there too. And why is she playing with the sleeves of her sack so much? Reaching in and then folding them higher and higher . . . ?

Eventually, she thanks everyone for their participation, and people go back to their sleeping areas. I watch as Liliana rearranges her blanket and talks to Isa in hushed tones. Liliana seems to be very preoccupied with one of the tattered sacks they make us wear in here. It looks like she somehow got hold of a needle and thread and is now the resident seamstress too.

I make my way over to Liliana and ask, "What are you doing?"

"Oh, poor Isa was tripping over her sack," she tells me. "So I was able to get another one, and I'm sewing a hem."

"How'd you get another sack? And a needle and thread?"

Liliana blinks slowly. Her eyes are still so warm and kind, it's hard for me to feel mad at her.

"I . . . have a few helpers." She smiles at Isa, who in turn smiles at me. "I hope you will rejoin us in prayer soon," Liliana says. She takes me in her arms, and I want to dissolve again, but I can't. It's like my body is too parched and hardened to even get to my tears. I just hold Liliana as she cries. Then Isa joins in, hugging my waist.

"I miss Señorita Kenna too," she says. I can hear the tears catching in her throat, and then she bawls, hard. This poor child. No one this young should have to bear the weight of all this grief. I hold them both until we all are on the edge of sleep. We say good night long after the cage lights have been turned off for the night.

Still, the next day, I can't help wondering about that sack Liliana was sewing and the strange things she was doing with her sleeves. I keep replaying the prayer circle in my head. I keep seeing that woman with the boils stepping forward with a shaky fist . . .

I have a name too!

Me too! And me!

Something about those women feels put on—not that I doubt they are desperate for relief and have people they miss and true, heartfelt prayers to share. But there's something so unusual about the way they got up one by one and insisted on holding Liliana's hand for so long. The women in our cage were usually too debilitated—physically or mentally—to stand up, let alone touch someone else's blistered, stinging skin. Why were these women all of a sudden so eager to press their hands into Liliana's?

That night, I skip dinner again. Not to meet Kenna, of course. Not to do anything remotely pleasurable or with any glimmer of joy.

This time, I'm skipping my evening meal to spy. I get back to our cage before everyone else and go straight to Liliana's sleeping area. She is always meticulous about folding her scratchy blanket in the morning, making it neat and flat so that if the officers sweep through, there's nothing to look at or disturb. But I can already see that her space looks a little different today. The sack that she was "mending" last night is folded between her blanket and her metal pallet. I unfold it quickly to get a better look, and I hear a clinking sound. It feels heavier than our usual flimsy sacks.

Is there something inside of it? I turn it inside out and start inspecting the hem that Liliana's made. It's not quite finished yet, but the part that she's sewn is filled with something. Or a lot of small somethings that feel almost like tiny pebbles.

Could it be *aqualinium*?

When Liliana finds me with her mysterious sewing project in my hands a few minutes later, I'm not exactly surprised. But she looks shocked and a bit scared.

"What is this?" I demand.

"Oh, I was doing some mending. It's nothing." She smiles and tries to take the sack out of my hands, but I hold it close to my ribs.

"If it's nothing, why do you want it so badly?"

She reaches for it again. As I grip it even tighter, I feel a bit of aqualinium brush my leg and fall to the ground.

Liliana scrambles to pick it up, then looks at me with pleading eyes.

"Please, Rania. Give it back."

There are more and more women coming in from dinner. The children will be here soon too, I know. And then neither of us will have a chance to talk or explain anything without a few dozen ears listening.

"I promise. It is nothing that you need to worry about," Liliana says. Her voice is soft but direct.

"I'm not worried," I tell her. "But I do need to know what you're doing."

"Just please be sure to keep hoping. To keep looking after

Isabel. And to keep . . . yes. Just do what I tell you, and it will be okay."

"What are you talking about?"

She's not making sense now, and the cage is getting more crowded.

Isa runs in and hugs my legs. "You're joining us for escuela tonight?" she asks. Then, without waiting for an answer, she shouts to the other children, "Come, come. It's time for escuela!"

"*Please*," Liliana says to me again. "Give me back my things and it will be okay."

The children are gathering in the middle of the cage and starting to clear small patches of dirt so they can write. The officers are circling outside, announcing the last call for the outhouse before the cages are locked and the night shift begins. And Liliana is waiting, holding her hands out to me so I can return this sack lined with bits of aqualinium.

"It will be okay," she repeats.

I don't believe her at all. But I give her back the sack and watch the children. Because what else can I do?

VALI

All I want to do is tear through these canyons and smash open those camp gates. I have fantasies of charging into the camps with guns and bombs. I have a clear image of me clasping Mami's hand as we run through walls of fire. I don't know if Mami is in that camp for sure. I saw a glimpse of something. It was just a fleeting vision, a shadowy figure that I saw from the top of a train. I was delirious with thirst and longing. But I need to set those people free because *somebody's* mami is in there. Possibly mine.

I feel like I'm suffocating as I lie on my bed inside the barracks. The slot canyon walls are like a vise closing in on my body. I need to get out of here. My thoughts are on a loop. Mami, aqualinium, bombs, guns, freedom, Officer Belton, chip in his wrist, eye scans, downloading files, escape, and Mami again. I'm not sleeping much even though Dre is constantly telling me I need to sleep to be on my A game.

"You're not a machine, González," he warns me.

"You've said that already . . . like a thousand times," I shoot back.

"Well, when you sleep, soldier, I'll stop reminding you."

He's a good leader. He's kind, confident, decisive, and disciplined. I feel safe with him at the helm. I think he'll make the right decisions, as hard as they might be when we're in the middle of some shit.

Vero and I have really bonded too. I've slowly started to open up to her. She's kind and generous. I can see us becoming really good friends. I didn't know how much I missed having a girl to talk to and hang out with. Ever since the world broke open, it's been me, Ernie, and Malakas. Don't get me wrong, I love them both, but Ernie is my little brother, and things with Malakas are just complicated right now. We can't hologram each other, and writing emails is almost impossible due to the constant surveillance of the Other 49. We can't do anything to reveal our location, so we take extra precautions with all of our communications, which means we hardly talk to our loved ones. The few times I have gotten to speak on the satellite phone with him, I feel like there is some kind of tension between us. Our words and our silence are filled with thorns and feelings we can't share with each other. I can't tell him about Operation Tempest, so whenever he asks me about work, I have to lie to him. I hate lying to him, but if he knew I was keeping something from him, I know things would be even worse. Before I became a Condor, I shared everything with Malakas. He saved my life a million times, and I saved his just as many. When you save someone's life, boundaries kinda stop existing. Or at least they did between us, until SOLIS demanded something different of me.

I haven't told Vero about Malakas. I mean, she knows about him. But she doesn't know that we had—or maybe have—a thing. It's all so complicated. She knows how we got to California. To be honest, it seems like everyone here knows how we got to California. Whenever I'm introduced to someone, they say, "Oh yeah. You're the girl who escaped the DF by jumping in the river." I always nod with a tight smile. The river: that's what they know, but there was so much more than the river. The trains, the delirium in the desert, Tomás's drowning, Volcanoman being taken, Rosa's broken body, drones, the hunger, the thirst, Mami telling me to go. No one ever asks anything more. I'm just the girl who got to sanctuary, and now I'm a Condor.

Vero noticed how my shoulders got tight and my fists clenched whenever anyone said "Oh yeah, I heard about you . . ."

"These people don't know squat," she whispered under her breath as they walked away. It felt so good to be seen, but then instantly a pang of sadness slashed my heart. That's how I used to feel about Malakas. I felt seen, heard, and held. Now I feel like I'm floating without him in a sea of strangers.

My mantra doesn't give me much comfort these days either. I used to find focus and anger when I said the names of all the people the DF had taken from me, but now I feel anxiety and a tinge of fear. I'm not afraid of the DF. I'm afraid of not being able to do my job. I'm scared I'll mess up. I won't be able to get the files. I won't be able to protect the people of California. I'm scared I'll fail the President, General Choi, the people in the camps, Dre, Vero, Ernie, Mami. The list goes on and on. The fear is building. I can't talk about it with Malakas because I can't talk about Operation Tempest. I can't talk about it with Vero because if she sees my insecurities, she won't want me on the mission. I know if someone was as weak as I am, I'd kick them off the mission. I wouldn't want them on the team because their weakness would put us all in danger. *Oh my God, am I a danger to everyone? Am I going to be the one who makes us fail?* My mind is spiraling. The questions dig me deeper and deeper into despair.

Nothing is impossible with faith and love, I hear Mami's voice whisper to me. But I'm having so much trouble finding faith and love right now. The saddest part is, I know that if I could just sound it all out with Mami, then she would be able to put all these pieces into place.

This is what she did with my homework, this is what she did when I had meltdowns, this is what she did my whole life. Sitting at our little table in the kitchen, surrounded by her altars to La Virgen, she cut through all my worries and confusion, my fogs of fear or uncertainty. She always found a way forward, even leading me and Ernie to California after she was taken by the DF. She was always telling us that if we looked hard enough, we would see miracles all around us. Usually,

Ernie and I just rolled our eyes or nodded to make her feel better, but now I feel like I'm hoping so desperately for her to be right. I wish she could give me a sign that she's alive and that this is the path forward.

I look up at the sky, in the rock walls, even down at my hands, searching for any hint of her presence.

"Vali, get up." Dre knocks on the door to my barracks. "Top dogs are waiting for us," he says.

I jump out of bed and put on my shoes.

"What do they want?" I ask.

"No clue. Find Vero and get to the council room ASAP."

He hollers Lisifrey's name down the hall. I hustle to the next room and grab Vero. We are at the leadership council room within minutes. The regulars are around the table. We've been here so many times now, all the formalities are gone. We've been waiting for our agent in the camp to give us the green light to go in for weeks.

We are as prepared as we can be. We know our advantages and disadvantages. There are a lot of disadvantages with regards to the terrain. We don't have a lot of cover as we approach the camp. We're in the middle of a desert, which leaves us exposed to the drones, to surveillance, to wild animals, and to bad weather. Our advantages are our training, the element of surprise, and our agent on the inside. The security system at the labor camp is almost impenetrable, but our hackers have been able to work miracles. They figured out a way to remotely cut off the wall's electricity. Once the mine explodes, our hackers will infiltrate the drone operating system and knock out all communications with the Other 49 headquarters and with the drones. While we are on our mission, SOLIS soldiers will attack and invade the other side of the camp. They will free as many prisoners as possible. There are an estimated five thousand prisoners inside the labor camp. SOLIS plans to transport them as quickly as possible back into California.

Everyone understands this part of the mission is perilous. Large Mack trucks will be filled to the brim with people. While anything is possible, we're banking on the surprise attack and the disruption of communications to buy enough time for the trucks to safely return to California.

I try to focus my mind on all the advantages we have, but I can't help but feel I am the biggest disadvantage.

"We've received word from our agent." General Choi looks around the room to each of us. "We are a go. You will leave here in one week. This is what we've been waiting for."

Everyone is quiet. I thought I would be thrilled when we got our go date, but instead I feel unmoored. I look at everyone in the room and see sadness in their eyes. Maybe because we know soon everything will change. Some of us may not even be here anymore.

"Go get your things in order, soldiers."

Even General Choi's voice holds a hint of heaviness.

As I walk out of the meeting, I look up at the sky. It's stained an orange pink as the sun dips behind the slot canyon walls. Sunsets have always felt like home to me. My first memory is of the setting sun in the mountains of Colombia. I was three or four, and I remember sitting on my father's lap as my mother cooked a sancocho alongside the river Ovejas. The fire embers burned underneath the large black pot. The chicken, potatoes, and corn cooked inside the bubbling soup. The smell of sancocho swirled around us. The sky was painted a light lavender, the edges of the mountain glowed amber, and Mami and Papi laughed at something I had done. I remember the feeling of home and safety nestled among us. The moment was perfect. A handful of months later, the three of us started walking north to the United States, and I've never felt anything close to that safety since. But sunsets remind me that I can find a home and I will be safe again.

LILIANA

I think I need to give Rania something to hold on to. I think it's time to share the plan with her. It might allow her heart to start to mend.

I walk to Isa, who is drawing in the dirt with the other kids. I kneel down in front of her.

"Isa, let's play a game!"

"Okay, Lili!" she squeaks.

"Let's see how long you can keep all the kids away from me and Rania. I am going to be counting. Let's try and get to one hundred seconds!"

"Okay!" She runs off and corrals the kids to the opposite end of the cage.

I walk to Rania. She looks up at me with annoyance and anger in her eyes.

"Let's talk about the dress," I say.

I sit down on her bunk. I take my hands in hers. I know this will not be easy for Rania. It was extraordinarily destabilizing to me when Nelini told me about SOLIS. I whisper as quickly and quietly as I can.

"Please don't repeat anything I say."

She nods in agreement.

"It wasn't fair for me to keep this from you. I wanted to tell you from the beginning, but I didn't think you were ready. You have always been on my mind and in my heart for everything."

She nods, a bit confused. I take a deep breath and continue.

"The sack you found is part of a plan to get us out of here. People have been bringing me aqualinium. I'm sewing a hem and putting it inside. I'm going to use it . . . as a bomb."

Rania's eyes widen.

Now that I am saying these words out loud, I wonder, how can this possibly work? A dress as a bomb? What if the aqualinium isn't actually an explosive? How much aqualinium do we need? I start to spiral.

"It's— It's going to be hard," I say, trying to ease my own doubts. "But we can do it. I really think we can. I have a lighter too. And we aren't doing this alone. There's a resistance group called SOLIS."

And then, for the first time in days, Rania looks at me with an emotion besides fury or anguish. She stares at me with those wide, plaintive eyes. Her mouth is twisted in a deep confusion and maybe a hint of curiosity.

"Who the fuck is SOLIS?" she asks.

"Shhh. Please. They're people who want to help us. It's a group that's fighting against the DF and the Other 49. They're going to be here when—" I look around to make sure no one is listening to us. Isa is playing Follow the Leader with the younger kids and keeping them on the other side of the cage. For a brief second, I imagine Isa in a real school, on a real playground, playing with her friends. Her mom is sitting on a park bench with a bag full of snacks.

I look back to Rania.

"They will be here when we—when I do the thing."

I haven't said these words out loud. They've just lived in my head on a constant loop. I believe words have power, and these ones especially.

Rania is relentless with her questions. For every detail I give her, she has a reason it won't work. I let her sound them all out and try not to get upset, but at a certain point I know my voice is sharp when I say, "Are you done? Because I—we—are going to do this, whether you believe in it or not."

Rania rolls over without saying a word. A few seconds later, the night-shift workers are called to the mine. The kids scurry back to their beds. Isa looks over at me to see how she's done. I give her two thumbs up as I walk to my bunk. She comes into my bed and nestles into my arms. I kiss her good night. The lights snap off.

The darkness envelops us. Our only companion is the icy-blue glow in each of our wrists.

Mi'ja, this night is so terribly hard. I don't know what to think anymore. Am I a fool to believe in this scheme? Am I an idiot to have faith in the goodness of people? The night is long and dark.

✖

THIS MORNING'S HARVEST is beyond my imagination. The clouds swell and churn; they sort of molt into a pea-green color and crackle loudly. We wait for the drops to fall, for the chosen victims to shriek in pain and die. But instead, there is water.

There are no sobs or tears or calls for revenge, and somehow it is even scarier that way.

They finally did it.

They made it rain.

The DF officers are hooting and hollering in triumph; they blare the national anthem at full volume from every speaker. We, the prisoners, just stand there in shock. This is the moment everyone was killed for. The dead flash before my eyes. Their last moments on this Earth play in a rapid montage in my mind. I feel sick to my stomach. At the same time, I have to wonder, does this mean we will no longer be slaughtered? Have we survived? I am ashamed to admit relief rushes through my body.

I watch one DF officer belt out the national anthem. His face is hidden behind his mask, his body wrapped in a biohazard suit. He sings so hard his spit splatters against the clear shield in his mask. My relief turns to dread.

Now that the Other 49 can make it rain at their behest, what else will they be able to control? Will other countries give in to the Other 49's hateful desires? Their rule over the clouds, their command over the rain, their power over aqualinium makes their domination borderless. In actuality, the slaughter is far from over. It will only increase. It seems like it will be never-ending.

I look to Rania. She has tears streaming down her face. She knows what I know. She mouths a single word at me.

SOLIS.

Regardless of her doubts or of mine, this is the only plan we have now.

I spend the entire day numb. In the kitchen, I chop, stir, and boil on autopilot. Once dinner is served, I make my way back to our cage. I want nothing more than to find Rania sitting on my pallet, ready to plan our next steps. As I walk in, she is exactly where I was hoping she would be. We fall into each other's arms. I am all she has left in this world. She is all I have left in this camp. And together we are going to set people free.

"According to SOLIS, aqualinium is an explosive. If

we get enough aqualinium in that dress and set it on fire inside the mine, it can blow the entire thing up," I explain to her.

"Okay . . ."

"SOLIS also said that for the whole mine to blow up, we need to have methane accumulate inside of it."

"Methane? Like the gas?" asks Rania.

"Yes, if enough accumulates, then it will easily blow up."

"So how do we make that happen?"

"They didn't say. We have to figure that part out ourselves."

Rania is crestfallen.

"I know. I know it seems impossible and crazy. But we do not have another choice. This is the plan. We have to make it work because we don't have that much time."

"Okay. We will make it work," she says.

I love this child so much. I only want to protect her from the horrors of this place, and the only way to do that is to get out of here.

"Tell me everything about the mine. Describe every detail to me," I beg.

And she does. With each description, I see Rania coming back into herself. She starts to believe in this crazy and beautiful dream of liberation. I can see the spark of hope growing inside of her, and it is a beautiful sight to behold.

Rania tells me about the long tunnels that twist and turn in the dark. The glowing green aqualinium that is sprinkled in the walls, giving the facade of beauty but that is in actuality a deadly poison. She tells me about crawl spaces that are just big enough for her to lie down in. She talks about the bins for aqualinium that are placed in various parts of the mine. They are as big as dumpsters, and by the time a shift ends, they are filled to the brim with bits of the glittering mineral. She explains how there aren't that many DF officers in the mine. A handful at the entrance. A few walking around keeping an eye on the prisoners as they work. No one wants to be down there breathing in the toxic fumes, even in biohazard suits; the air is poisonous and nothing can truly protect you. She says the mine is empty of people when the shifts change. She talks about her mining tools. A small pickaxe, a hammer, and a headlamp. I ask her how they eat. She says they don't. How do they go to the bathroom? In the darkest corners. Nothing she tells me gets us any closer to figuring out how to make the methane build up. We talk until our minds are all twisted up, until our eyes lose the battle with sleep. The following night, we meet again. And still nothing. The following night again. And still no answers.

Doubt is starting to creep into my heart, mi'ja. The women keep on bringing me handfuls of aqualinium that I sew into the special burlap. The sack is filled with it. But we do not have a way to make the methane accumulate. To make matters even worse, Rania has started to cough. It's not as bad as Kenna's cough or Nelini's cough, but it is there.

Rania describes the mine to me again. She starts coughing. It begins as a tickle in her throat, but soon she sounds like she is hacking up a lung. I give her the only salve I have for miners' cough: a piece of ginger. She sucks on it for a bit. Once she stops coughing, I ask her, "Is it hard for you to breathe down there with this cough?"

"Sometimes. But they have a couple of these plastic-looking tubes running along the bottom with little fans. I think they bring air into—"

We turn to each other, wide-eyed.

"They bring air into the mine!" she blurts out.

"If air is coming in, then air has to be going out too," I say.

"If we stop the air from going out, the methane won't come out either. And if the methane doesn't come out . . ."

I hug Rania so hard. She is brilliant. I tell her that she is saving us all and that she will find love again. That anything and everything will be possible when she gets out of here!

For the first time since my arrival, I find myself

excited about the future. On this night, I am no longer filled with dread or fear. Instead, my heart brims with enthusiasm for our plan. I imagine the mine erupting in a spectacular explosion, flames soaring into the sky. Exhilaration washes over me as I picture the DF retreating in terror. Tears of joy well up in my eyes at the thought of Mishi and Esteban accompanied by their mothers, walking away from this camp, hand in hand, toward liberation.

I imagine Isa learning to write on a piece of paper instead on a patch of dirt. My heart clenches. I must find someone to take care of Isa because I won't be able to leave with her.

Mi'ja, there is no easy way to say this. I cannot soften the blow or lessen the pain.

I am so sorry.

I will not see you on the other side of these walls. I will not walk beyond this desert. I will not make it to California.

There is only one way to make the mine explode. I must wear the dress down into the mine. I must light it on fire. I must ignite the bomb.

I know I promised you and Ernesto we would be together again. Forgive me for failing you. I believe one day you will understand that I was forced to make an impossible choice. A life in this death camp is no life at all. I chose to fight back, to find freedom in my resistance, to find liberation in the emancipation of others.

To be your mother is to love so deep there is no end to it. To unfurl and widen, to see the world anew through your eyes. To have my love stretch and wrap itself to the past, present, and future you.

To be your mother, Vali, to be Ernesto's mother, has been and will always be my greatest honor.

RANIA

When I witnessed those first drops of artificial rain falling from the sky, I knew we were finished. The clouds gathered thick and tight, hovering over the harvest cage in a brownish-green haze. They sounded like they were crackling and steaming. And then they released big sizzling drops of liquid.

The prisoners in the cage cried out, as they always did. I started crying too. But as the first drops landed on their skin, they did not burn or melt.

They stayed alive.

Then the ground below them turned dark. Wet. I think every single person watching was stunned into silence.

Until a loud whooping sound came from the DF megaphones.

"Holy shiiiit!" one of the officers shouted. "It's fucking raining!!!"

Of course, as I stood there, caught between amazement and horror, the first thing I thought was, if only Kenna was picked for harvest *today*, she'd still be here. We would still be able to dream. I would climb through a thousand tunnels full of sewage with her and never let her go. If only . . .

But it wasn't her. It was a dozen new victims, who were slowly lowered and released from the cage. They were confused and breathless, but intact. And I had a new realization. Yes, the rainfall was small and already evaporating, so it wasn't a complete success, but there was no doubt that this was a major breakthrough for the DF. Manufacturing harmless rain like this would be a game changer for the New American Republic—and the entire world. If the New American Republic really had discovered a way to create viable rainfall, they would solidify their place as a global superpower.

And that meant . . . what would happen to us, the prisoners mining their aqualinium?

Or to California, our only chance at sanctuary?

Honestly, I didn't have many hopes for planting trees and eating mangoes in California anymore. I didn't have anyone left to share that or to plot out a future with. But as the DF erupted into a victorious encore of the anthem and people scattered around to look at the small puddles collecting, I spotted Isa—splashing.

Again, it wasn't a lot of rain, but it was enough to amaze a child who'd been thirsty and trapped here for so long.

Most likely, she had no idea that this rain could be her death sentence—that if we didn't get out of here now, we might never get another chance. And so, Isa is the reason I joined Liliana's plan. Isa is why I mouthed the word *SOLIS* and then described all the tunnels and crawl spaces to Liliana, wracking my brain for a way to unleash an explosion.

And Isa is holding my hand now, as I stand in line for my shift in the mine. I say goodbye to Isa and watch her go with the other children to clean out the officer barracks. But I think of her the whole day, as I scout out exactly where each of those ventilation fans are, attached to their rinky-dink tubing that I guess keeps us from suffocating.

This crazy plan is the only way Isa can possibly have a future.

I start doing some recon, trying not to get too obsessed with the fact that we have just a handful of days to figure this out. I grab my tools and go through every tunnel and crawl space that I can find. The darker the better—that way there are fewer prying DF eyes. I only find a handful of ventilation tubes, and they're pretty primitive. They're made of some flimsy vinyl-looking material, and from what I can tell, the little fans attached to them are always whirring. But if I can puncture the tubing somehow, maybe I can "dismantle" them, or at least disrupt the air flow.

When I report back to Liliana with this news, she is giddy, clapping her hands and whispering, "Yes, yes!"

I keep telling her I'm not sure how or if it will work. I

remember enough chemistry to know that methane is a colorless, odorless gas. So there's really no way to know if there's enough buildup for it to be flammable.

"Please," Liliana urges. "Just do the best you can. And trust."

Easier said than done.

There are probably a half dozen tubes snaking into the mine, and just as many DF officers stationed in there too. They roam around every hour or so, making sure we stay busy and collect our aqualinium deposits. There's also a team of them lurking at the top of the mine, not to mention other prisoners whom I don't want to get in trouble.

I try to remind myself that I know this space all too well. I could navigate these rancid tunnels and passageways while blindfolded if needed. Sometimes, when people have gotten sick from the heat and stench, or gotten beaten for being "lazy," I actually have worked with my eyes closed. It was the only way I knew to keep going and not get brutalized myself. I also know which of these craggy walls are sturdiest, and which are probably a few blows away from crumbling.

Actually, I remember a crawl space that did collapse on two prisoners a few months ago, leaving one dead and the other paralyzed. When I shut my eyes, I can still hear the sounds of those rocks groaning and then crashing on the women's bodies. They were two sisters, I think. The crack of their bones echoed all around us; their shrieks scraped at the sky.

I decide to go to that collapsed section first. Here at least I know there won't be many people. The walls are too unstable, and I think even the DF officers down here are a little scared of it. But behind one of the jagged rock piles, I see a small dented fan. And winding its way from the fan toward some of the rubble is a gray vinyl tube.

Yes! I clutch my pickaxe and try to stab through the tubing. The point is so dull, it practically bounces off. On my second attempt, the ax slips from my hands and clatters to the ground.

"Problem handling the tools?" one of the DF officers growls.

"Sorry," I mutter, and get busy chipping away at a ridged outcropping that glints with flecks of aqualinium. The officer sort of lingers nearby for what feels like hours. He doesn't even take a water break or switch places with anyone. I'm scared my shift will end without me getting to destroy a single piece of tubing, and then what will Liliana say?

I try to move around while still keeping that fan and tubing in sight. At one point, I take a huge swing and hammer into one of the rocks so hard that a big slab falls off, just missing my leg. A shelf of thick dirt starts sliding down around me, and I can hear the officer on my tail retreating, muttering curse words.

Aha!

I have probably less than a minute to get down and puncture that tube before a tide of rocks and debris falls on my head. I slam the spade through the vinyl and pull it out as fast as I can, scrambling out just as the rocks start cascading.

"Watch it!" the officer barks at me. "From now on, you're

over there!" He grabs the back of my neck as if I'm a disobedient dog, then hurls me toward another crosscut that has a sturdier-looking pitch. It also has two officers patrolling, so I don't know how I'm going to puncture another tube on this shift, but I still feel a little bit victorious.

"I think I disabled one," I tell Liliana that night.

"One?" she asks. She bites her lip, and I can tell she's disappointed. Or maybe doubt is creeping in—this is a complicated plan after all. "Okay, this is a start," she says. "This is good. But . . . we don't have much time."

"It's harder than I thought," I explain.

"Yes. You did a good job. It's just . . . did you see the drone malfunction at the harvest today?"

"You mean the one that fell from the sky?" I ask.

"Yes. That was SOLIS's signal." Liliana sighs. "They are in position and will be here tomorrow night."

"Tomorrow night?!"

This totally changes everything. There's no more time to stake out the most overlooked corner or edge my way toward the nearest fan. There is no time to tie up loose ends or say any goodbyes.

"And so . . . what do we do?" I ask.

"Well, during your morning shift tomorrow, if you can poke more holes, that will be wonderful, and then . . . when it's time for the explosion, you will be in charge of Isa. And then . . ." Liliana's eyes glimmer with tears, but she nods them away. "Then we just trust."

I try not to think about all the loopholes and what-ifs. Like, how will SOLIS get all of us out of here? And how will we know there's enough methane to cause a chemical reaction? I never earned those science degrees my parents wanted me to go to college for, but even I know there are vital details missing from this experiment.

And surely, there's a catalyst that Liliana has never named, but all I know for sure: I think Liliana is planning to wear that sack full of aqualinium into the mine. Or maybe she will try to hide it somehow. Either way, when she lights it on fire, I think she will be taken by the flames.

Even as I imagine this, my body starts quaking with a wild heat. My eyes are watering as if I'm staring into those roaring flames; the smoke is shutting out everything that came before now.

And I know this. I *feel* this: I cannot let Liliana sacrifice herself. She has children who love her and need her, who I'm sure are searching for her desperately. Even though she's told me to take care of Isa, there's nothing I can offer that little girl if we do make it out of here alive.

I know this for sure. The biggest gift I could give to any of them is the possibility of freedom.

I am the only one who can actually make this plan work. I am the only one who knows these rocks inch by inch—their gradients and cracks, caverns and sinkholes. I am the only one who is ready to die for this cause because it would actually be a relief to feel like maybe, possibly . . .

I helped them find liberation.

I imagine Isa standing in front of a real classroom, proudly spelling out her name. I picture Mishi laughing with her mom on a park bench in the sun. I see rainbows and tomorrows and a lightness that Kenna and I dreamt of outside these walls.

I don't tell Liliana any of this, of course. Instead, I promise that I will trust and try to have faith.

All of which is true. And when I say this, Liliana gives me a hug that's so tight, I feel our heartbeats bouncing off each other, feeding each other for maybe the last time.

I don't sleep at all that night—my mind is frantic with plotting and planning. The next day, as soon as they lower us down for the morning shift, I make a beeline for the first fan I see without officers nearby. I charge toward it and attempt to spear the connecting tube as quickly and quietly as possible. Nothing happens. I try pinning down the tube with one hand and driving the rusty blade in with the other. A current of pain rushes through me as I see that I've made a hole in the webbing between two of my fingers instead of the equipment.

I chew the inside of my cheek to keep myself from moaning, and wipe the blood off on my sack.

"Everybody have a station?" The DF are about to fan out in every direction. I have maybe one more chance if I'm lucky. I take a last swing at the tube, and it collapses with a loud *ssh-waaa* sound. I spin around and do my best to create a distraction, hammering away at some loose rocks until a sprinkling of pebbles starts falling and pelting me.

"What the fu . . . ?"

Then I hear the snap of one of those disgusting robotic dogs as it grabs on to my sack and yanks me away from the tumbling rocks. The dog dumps me in front of two DF officers in the middle of the pit.

"You seem to be having a lot of trouble with your tools, huh?" one of the officers says. "Give 'em here." He opens a gloved palm, and I have no choice but to hand over my pickaxe and hammer. The robodog snarls just inches from my face.

"Yeah," the other officer says, circling around me slowly. "Let's cool it on the avalanches, huh? See what you can do with your hands."

"Get to it," the first officer adds. He kicks me in the shin with one of his steel-toed boots, and I crash into another mass of rocks, splitting my cheek open. But at least I know I've gotten another tube dismantled.

"Is two enough?" I ask Liliana when I get back. She insists on using the last drops of water in her cup to rinse out my wounds. She meets my gaze with her warm brown eyes and says, "You did brave work. Thank you. Thank you for everything." She takes in a deep sigh and hugs me again.

I am going to miss Liliana so much when I'm gone. I'm going to miss even the sting of my broken skin and the wracking coughs that seem to be coming faster with each passing day.

But either way, in just a few hours, it will all be over.

I've made my decision. I'm ready to go.

VALI

The six of us sit in silence in the back of a delivery truck as we drive across the desert. We are hidden to the outside world, but we are very much exposed to one another. We've made a promise to each other. We've committed our lives to one another. We have promised to fight to the death, to kill, to hurt, to do whatever it takes to get those files to SOLIS. We understand that at least one of us must come back. This reality terrifies me. Not the possibility of death, but rather the possibility of failure.

I flash back again to the ride Ernie and I trembled through last year. We were crammed in a meat truck with swinging carcasses and desperate souls. Everything felt so new and unknown then. I thought that was as bad as it could possibly get, but I was so very wrong.

We were runaways then.

Now I am a Condor.

The truck stops. The engine is shut off. It is completely silent outside. A strange calm comes over me. Everything feels eerily still. The back door opens. We slide into the desert. Each of us finds cover where we can: a barren bush, a small ditch, a rock. It's not pretty out here—the earth is cracked and covered in thick green-gray dust; the little bits of vegetation are charred and leafless. I hear birds gliding overhead.

We have been dropped off about fifteen miles away from the camp. This is the closest we can get without being detected by the Other 49's drones or security system.

We will walk through the night and arrive at the labor camp's electrified wall. A handful of hours to get to the location we will breach. Once there, we will wait for the mine to explode. As the chaos unfolds, we will retrieve the files and others will make sure the people are freed. Everything depends on the explosion.

If the explosion goes off.

If any of this works.

I couldn't call Malakas before I left. I know it was selfish, but there is too much stuck in my head and my heart. I knew that if I heard his voice, I'd burst open and spill all of my fears and doubts. I want to tell Malakas that I think about his sad eyes way too much and can still feel our very first kiss. I want to tell Kenna I love her and I'd do anything for her. I want to tell Papi that he didn't die in vain and that he gave me the strength to fight. I want to tell Mami that I'm doing the best I can, that I'm trying to trust and believe. That even when there is nothing to hold on to, I'm doing everything in my power to hold on. Maybe this is what she means by faith. Maybe this moment before I head out into the unknown is my first and last prayer.

JESS

When Rania comes toward me that evening at dinner, my first reaction is fear. I'm fearful because I know she hates me and all that I represent. And for the first time in maybe my entire life, I don't blame her.

"Hey. What's your name again?" she asks.

"Jess."

"Right. Jess." She gives me a long once-over, but her eyes don't seem hateful. They just look tired. "Well, I need you to do something for me, Jess."

"Yeah! Sure!" It's a little sad how eager I am to please her. Especially when I have nothing to offer.

"After dinner, I'm going to take your shift in the mine."

"Oh . . . kay." I don't know why she's doing this, but of course I say yes.

"And you're going to do escuela with the kids. Isa will show you how it's done."

"She's so sweet."

Rania stiffens a little when I say that. It looks like she may be blinking back tears. "Yeah. She's a good kid," Rania continues. "Whatever happens, you have to keep your eye on her. You have to make sure she's okay."

"Sure. Okay. Do you want me to take one of your shifts tomorrow, then, or maybe . . . ?" I don't know what I'm proposing, but Rania ignores me anyway. She is urgent and focused, listing all the songs that help Isa get to sleep at night and telling me to gently remind Esteban to use the outhouse when he can.

"Yes, yes," I keep repeating, nodding until I feel dizzy. Rania has so many instructions for this one night. And she makes me swear not to tell a soul about any of this. I have no idea why anyone could possibly want another shift in that hellhole, but my skin is stinging just thinking about it.

Before I can thank her or ask what this is all about, Rania turns and weaves her way into another group of prisoners.

I'm left staring at my empty food tray and listening to the stupid New American Republic anthem they always pipe in and play on loop while we're eating.

From the mountaintops
To the pristine shores
We shall fight for justice
Truth forevermore

I had no idea what those words actually meant when I first heard them. I was just regurgitating all the bullshit that I'd learned in grade school. But that doesn't excuse me from any of this.

It's my fault that I signed up to be part of this genocide.

It's my fault that thousands of people are being sacrificed to make fake rain fall from the sky.

It's my fault that I never stopped to question or consider how we are all made of blood and bones, hungers and thirsts.

This is what I want to tell Rania even though I know that it won't help anyone. It won't bring back her dead girlfriend or any of the lives lost in this horror show. I don't know how I can fix any of this now. I don't know if it will ever be fixed.

So I just let her go.

RANIA

The time is here. The time is now.

I scoop most of my dinner onto Isa's and Esteban's dinner plates and tell them to chew slowly, because that's what I usually do. As I turn to go, Isa says, "I have a new song for escuela tonight."

I feel my neck tighten and my face flush with guilt.

"I can't wait," I tell her, even though I know I'll be in the mine by then.

What I wish I said is "I love you, sweet girl. I *believe* in you. Now, be brave. Be loud. When you get out of here, please keep singing. Keep dancing and laughing and writing and drawing. You can do this. It *is* possible."

I'm not sure exactly how I've gotten to this place of calm. But I do know that ever since I've committed to walking into the mine and starting the fire, I've felt a deep sense of relief. It's almost joyful. Because for the first time in what feels like eons, I am not just scrabbling to survive; I'm taking action. Mama always wanted me to be quiet and keep the peace, but whose peace was I keeping by following orders here?

I can't keep silent and wait for someone else to end this. I have to. I want to. I am stepping into the unknown and blasting open a new path—for Isa and Esteban, for Mishi and Liliana. Even Jess, if she's smart enough to follow.

I walk by with my head down and head to our sleeping quarters.

There's an officer stationed outside our tent. "Didn't like the salad bar?" he scoffs. Because to him, this is all a game and my life has always been a mistake.

I keep my eyes glued to the ground and do not answer. For a brief moment, I let myself imagine what it might look like for this man to watch the mining pit explode. I picture him running through the smoke, unleashing bullets into the air. He doesn't know what he's shooting at or where he's headed. It's *his* turn to be on the run.

When I get inside our cage, there are just a few people there, all of them crumpled in despair or trying to sleep off whatever horrors the day brought. I go straight to Liliana's sleeping area and pull back the edge of her blanket. I find the special sack that she's hemmed and lined with aqualinium. Then I quickly pull off the one that I'm wearing and replace it for hers, covering it with her blanket again. As I wriggle my body into Liliana's masterpiece, trying not to disturb any of the glittering pebbles, I think of the navy-blue dress that Mama bought me for my middle school graduation. This was back when we lived in Chicago. She hated shopping, but she went and picked out this little thing with buttons down the front and puffy sleeves. I told her that it was too itchy and I'd only wear it if I was going to a funeral.

I'm sorry, Mama, I say to myself. *I'm sorry I never showed you the love and appreciation you deserved. I'm sorry you waited in line at the department store and I never thanked you.*

Now, as I stand tall in Liliana's special burlap sack, it feels a thousand times worse on my skin, like an itch climbing down into my bones. And yet it also feels magical. Or at least that's what I tell myself as I try to slow my racing heartbeat. I feel for the spot in the sleeve where she's sewn in a finger-sized lighter, and suck in a deep breath.

"Goodbye, my friends," I mumble. I gaze around this fetid cage. This is where I held Mama for the last time. This is where I leaned into Kenna's shoulder and felt a shimmer of *can this be?* This is where I heard Mishi speak her name and Liliana list the dead and so many of us cry out for salvation.

If this plan doesn't work—if I just burn to death in the bottom of the mine or the officers use me for target practice, I hope Liliana doesn't linger too long on my name or blame herself.

This is *my* choice. I am ready to say goodbye.

When I walk back outside to get ready for the night shift, I see a hazy silhouette of the moon hanging above the horizon. It's just a slice of the moon really. A crooked yellowish grin, dipping in and out of clouds.

"Awoooo," I whisper into the air. Because Kenna and I used to howl at the moon together whenever we caught a glimpse of it.

It felt like some sacred jewel in the sky—an artifact from another lifetime. Kenna loved the moon, and I did too, and we were going to follow it together. We were always going to be together.

Maybe that's still possible. Sure, I was brought up to believe in science and only facts that can be proven under a microscope. But I have to believe in something beyond our human understanding. Maybe I get to come back to life as an elephant or a tree. Maybe I get absorbed into the wind or echo like a star. Either way, there's no harm in fantasizing about Kenna being there too. Mama and Baba too. I get to give myself at least that dream.

The night shift gets lowered into the mine without a sound. It's much colder in here after dusk. I try not to shiver because I know every bit of aqualinium is held in by just a few stitches. The floodlights are on now, but they seem to create more shadows than light as the crater rises up around us on every side, cracked and ominous.

We disembark and turn on our headlamps.

"Remove the cage!" yells one of the DF officers.

Nothing happens.

"Remove the cage!" orders another officer, this time through a large megaphone. We need the cage to be removed so we can spread out to dig.

I follow the DF officer's voice up to the top of the mine to see who is in charge of the cage. There's a small posse of officers up there, but not a single one is paying attention to us. Instead, there are two mechanical canines growling and people scurrying around. It looks like a prisoner is getting pulled away from the edge of the pit.

I let out an audible gasp when I realize who it is: Liliana. I can't see her face fully in this light, but I know her small frame, the way she lists to one side and shakes her head when she is deep in thought.

I think she knows what I am about to do.

"It's okay," I whisper. Maybe for her. Maybe for myself. And then I watch as the DF drag her away.

✖

THE NIGHT SHIFT is supposed to go from seven in the evening until three in the morning so everyone can be present for the morning roll call and harvest selection. I try to take in every minute of this experience. I don't reach for any tools. Instead, I really *feel* my blistered skin touching sharp rock, the nerve endings sending a message to my brain that this hurts, my breath stopping for a beat as I process the sting and then releasing. It's amazing what the human body can endure. And how easily we can decide that one kind of human is more worthy of life than another.

When the DF officers call all of us in for final collection, I'm honestly surprised. I had no idea time could move that quickly. As everyone lines up to give their aqualinium deposits, I duck into one of the darkened tunnels to wait.

I listen to the buckets get filled, to the clink of small pebbles that hold so much power. I listen to the human cargo being loaded onto the cage, to the sighs and coughs floating up into the sky. I listen to my heart, fast but steady. Counting down the moments until it is time.

I do not come out until the floodlights are turned off and the 3:30 A.M. sirens blare through the tents. Esteban must be rubbing the sleep out of his weary eyes. Maybe Isa is tugging on Liliana's sleeve, like she does every morning.

As for me, it is not morning or night, beginning or end. It is a single flick of the lighter. A touch of the flame to this scratchy hem. My pulse is throbbing through every inch of my skin. I tell myself it is okay. I am ready to give up this body, this existence, to let myself splinter open into embers and stars. Maybe each piece of me can ignite another fire, and another. Until we are a roaring flame that breaks open the sky and demands a new beginning.

The smoke is getting so thick now. My lungs are blazing; my eyes are blinded as everything around me blasts a searing yellow. I hear a deafening explosion, and I start singing Kenna's song . . .

Eh soom boo kawaya
Kedou, kadee
Eh soom boo kawaya
Kedou, kadeeeee

I am no longer bound to this Earth. I feel myself getting lighter and lighter, rising to the sky amid the orange, red, yellow, blue. My arms spread like wings, and my legs disappear completely. I am no longer holding my breath. I am inside my breath, traveling through to the other side. Soon, I will be just wisps of smoke, or a handful of ashes that drift and sail without ever needing a home.

I see Kenna in the distance. We are bits of ash floating on a soft current of air. We do not have to be anywhere or do anything. We are giddy with our formlessness, not knowing or caring where or how we exist. We are so much more than our physical bodies ever were. There is no struggle here—no scrabbling or scrambling or fighting just to exist. There is just this weightless peace. And as we float up, up, up, I hear Kenna's disembodied voice say, *Yes! Look what you've done!*

I imagine the flames blasting open the camp's wall. There are people running, shouting, crying, laughing.

I see Isa, Jess, and Liliana sprinting toward the opening, calling for everyone to follow them.

I see Mishi in her mother's arms as they charge into the desert.

I see little Esteban dribbling a soccer ball, getting faster and faster.

And behind him are five purple horses, three chickens, two goats, and his very own rainbow.

Because maybe it's all impossible, but also . . .

Anything can happen.

VALI

CRRRRRRAAAAACKKKKK!

The explosion announces the beginning and the end in a single deafening roar.

Everything is exploding. The earth, the sky, the staggering impossibility of this moment. What happens next is not only a miracle, it is also faith and courage, sacrifice and determination. It is a sudden hush so beautiful and profound. And then a soft *plink, plink, plinkplinkplink*. A shower of those now useless drones fall from the sky. We stay in position until the electric hum of the wall is gone too.

Silence.

Our hackers have done their job. Their infiltration is complete.

We slowly approach the wall. We pull out our rope-launching guns and shoot. The ropes zip out into the dark night, attaching to the top of the wall. Julian pulls himself up the forty-foot wall within seconds. He signals it's safe for us to climb it.

My adrenaline is pumping hard. I'm at the top of the wall just a few seconds later. I adjust my night vision glasses and . . .

I'm stunned.

There are people everywhere. Everyone looks starved and hunted. Some of them are so frail, I'm scared they'll snap in half. There is a lot of smoke from the explosion, and people are coughing so badly they can't even walk. I see a woman scoop up a little boy as she runs away from the smoke. Another woman lies on the ground with what looks like a shredded leg. My eyes well with tears. This is more gruesome than my nightmares. This is worse than I could have ever imagined. So many people. So much suffering. So much fear. I instinctively search for Mami. I need to find her.

"González! González!" Dre screams.

I snap back to what I am supposed to be doing. My job as a Condor. Not my job as a daughter.

"González! You good?"

"Yeah! Yeah . . . I'm good."

He looks at me, not entirely convinced but without any other options.

"Okay. Vero, Alan, González—stay close. Lisifrey—eyes on us the entire time. Julian, as soon as the target arrives, you stay on him. Make sure he stays alive. Let's go!"

We look at each other one last time before we break

apart. I have come to love each of them. Their commitment to California, to our people, to our freedom is unwavering. I know we will not fail each other.

We scale down the other side of the wall without being noticed. It's complete chaos on the ground. A huge fire roars at the other end of the camp. That must be where the mine exploded. There are sirens blasting. Rapid gunshots boom in the distance. Bloodcurdling screams fill my ears. I focus on Dre, who is weaving in between buildings, tents, and shadows. We dip behind a building as a group of DF officers run past us. Their radios blast out, "SOS! SOS! We need backup immediately at the mine! Everyone to the mine! NOW! NOW."

Are they fighting the fire, or has SOLIS invaded the camp already?

Pop!

I spin around, plant my feet, raise my rifle, and look through my viewfinder. I'm searching for the shooter. He's not shooting at us, but he's close to us.

Pop! Pop! Pop!

I zero in on the target. It's a DF officer. He's tall and burly-looking, pointing his gun at a group of people. Most of them are lying in their own blood. He points his gun at a woman who cowers underneath him. Her face is full of open sores. Her arms are as thin as twigs. Her brown hair reminds me of Mami. I put my finger on the trigger. The DF officer's head is in my crosshairs. I inhale, ready to pull the trigger on my exhale. I no longer care about Operation Tempest. All I care about is keeping this woman alive. Suddenly my viewfinder goes black. I look up and see Dre standing in front of my gun barrel.

"What the fuck are you doing?! You shoot him and then the entire DF force knows we're here!"

From behind Dre, I hear *pop!*

I blink back my tears. He's right. *What am I doing?* I'm going to get us all killed if I don't get it together. Dre turns toward the gunshot and spins around.

"Let's go! Don't look, González."

I don't have to. I know what that monster did. My only revenge now is to finish this mission.

We hide in the darkness and make our way to our target location. In the distance, we see a long line of huge gray tents. Through the smoke and chaos, I see people running out of them. They run away from us. I hope they are running toward freedom.

We hear a lot of gunfire at the other end of the camp. Other members of SOLIS must be engaging in direct combat with the DF by now. I'm happy Malakas is stationed in tech and development. I don't think I could handle him being in the middle of all of this.

We arrive at the computer hub without being seen. Our location is exactly as it appeared in the images. A small brick building with no windows and one door. Just as our intel told us, there is an officer at the door. He is heavily armed and in full-body gear. We knew there would always be an officer on duty. The Other 49 must protect whatever information is in that room at all costs. What they didn't expect was the officer would be their weak link. We are here to make sure their weakest link serves us.

The officer is agitated. I can tell he's nervous. He knows something is very wrong with this night, but he doesn't know what is coming for him. This officer doesn't have the chip we need to access the room, but we will use him to get what we need.

Dre whispers into his earpiece, "Condors, I'm approaching the target. Cover me."

"Yes, sir," we respond. I am only about fifty feet from Dre, hiding between dumpsters, but he feels miles and miles away.

I aim my gun right at the officer's head. He has on what looks like an impenetrable helmet, but if anything goes wrong, it's my only option. I keep my finger on the trigger and breathe as slowly and evenly as I possibly can.

Dre slides toward the officer. The officer doesn't notice Dre as he slips behind him. He quickly puts the officer in a headlock and brings his knife to his neck. Dre tells him to drop his gun. At first he refuses, but Dre digs his blade into his neck and the officer does as he's told. I can see a little blood trickle down his throat. I keep the officer in my crosshairs as Dre drags him into the dark.

"Vero, Lisifrey, Alan—eyes on camp. Vali, come here."

I get to the back of the building without anyone noticing me. Dre takes the butt of his rifle and smashes it on the officer's forehead. His helmet tumbles off of him as he falls to the ground. Dre pounds him in the face a few more times and kicks him hard in the chest. The officer whimpers in pain. He can barely breathe.

"González, hold him up." I do as I'm told. I grab him by his arms and jerk him up. He's like putty in my hands. His arms are so bony. I wonder why he's so skinny. Dre takes the officer's chin and pulls him close to his face. He's clearly scared. I don't think his DF training included how to keep it together when you're captured by the resistance. His blond hair is covered in dirt and blood. He has pimply skin and a little more than peach fuzz for a mustache. He's barely older than me.

"What's your name?"

"Henry." His voice cracks with emotion.

"Henry. You don't want to die here, right? Not in this crappy desert. Not like this, right?"

He shakes his head no.

"Good, cuz I don't want to hurt you. So, what I'm going to need you to do is call Officer Belton and tell him there's smoke coming out from under the door."

His eyes bulge as soon as he hears the words *Officer Belton*.

"No. Please. No."

"Yep. You're gonna call him. Now." Dre puts his knife under Henry's chin. He starts to dig into him again.

"Okay, okay . . . I'll do whatever you want. Just don't hurt me, okay? I need my radio."

"My partner here. She's going to put her gun to your temple. You say anything other than 'there's smoke coming out from under the door,' she'll shoot you. Got it?" Henry nods. I put the tip of my rifle on his temple. "You better sound normal too. Otherwise, you know what's gonna happen."

He nods again.

I pray to La Virgen, to Jesus, to mi Diosito lindo, *Please don't let him say anything else. Please don't let him try to be a hero. Please don't make me shoot this gun.*

Henry brings his wrist to his mouth and speaks into it. "Officer Belton," he says.

He sounds good, fairly normal, I think. I can't really tell. The world is so fucked up right now, it's hard for me to know what is up or down. For the past year all I've wanted is to hurt DF officers, but now that I might finally be able to do it, my body is in protest. My legs want to run away. My heart just wants to find Mami and escape into the desert so she can rock me to sleep like she used to do when I was a little girl.

"What?" crackles a very agitated voice from the officer's radio.

"Sir, there seems to be smoke coming from inside building 204. It's streaming out from under the door."

"What the— Is there a fire inside?"

"I don't know, sir. There's a lot of smoke coming from under the door. I can't tell what's going on inside."

"Stay guarding that door! I'm on my way."

"Yes, sir!"

Henry drops his head. I can see the shame rising inside of him.

"Good job, kid." Dre raises his gun and shoots him in the back of the head. I'm stunned. I knew this was always the plan, but seeing this guy's body in front of me, blood pooling around the hole in his head, makes me feel sick to my stomach. I feel myself wanting to float away. I struggle between staying present and being thrown into memory. I imagine all the people I've lost in the past year. I see Tomás. His small dead body in the lake. I see Rosa being taken by the drone. Her baby in her arms, and Tomás's corpse wrapped around her. Rosa, Tomás and her baby would still be alive if the Deportation Force hadn't hunted them. This person, this kid, would still be alive if we didn't have to become Condors. I look around the camp. This place wouldn't be here if the Other 49 never existed. All of this death, violence, and horror because they despise us. And now I am being sucked into their vortex of hate. They have taught me how to hate them. Mami would be so disappointed in me.

"González! González!"

Dre's voice forces me back to the present. I come back to him, to this camp, to this atrocity. My body is here, but my mind still lingers in the in-between.

"Help me with his clothes," Dre says.

My body is in motion. I don't have control over it. I'm like a zombie. We strip Henry of his uniform within seconds. Just as Dre puts on the DF uniform, Julian tells us that he has eyes on Officer Belton. He's coming with three other officers. This was always going to be our moment of surprise. We had no idea how many people would come with Officer Belton. We were hoping for two, but we can manage three. Vero's and Alan's voices come over the radio letting us know they are in position. Dre looks like he's full-on DF. He takes his position at the door. I get into my spot between the dumpsters across from our target building. I can't be seen, but I can see everyone. We all know the plan. On Dre's cue we will take out everyone except Officer Belton. He must stay alive at all costs.

My mouth is dry. It feels like I've been chewing on cotton. I feel like I'm floating away again, but I need to stay here. I need to stay present. I need to stay grounded. I try to say my mantra, but something is wrong. My mind is blank. I can't remember the names. I try to remind myself of my anger, my need for revenge, but there is nothing. My mouth stays dry, my hands tremble, my eyes can't focus.

Pop! Pop! Pop! Pop!

I look through the scope on my rifle. I move it right, left, up, and down. I don't see anything. The world is a blur. The shapes of buildings and tents are distorted. I am trying to figure out what's happening as gunfire explodes all around me. My earpiece blares with Julian's screams. "Dre is down. Dre is DOWN."

I see a body on the ground. He's in a DF uniform. Around him there are three more people. All in DF uniforms. All hurt, maybe dead? I can't tell which one is Dre. Everyone's face is hidden behind helmets and face shields.

"Where's our target?" I scream into the walkie. "Is he down?" I ask, dreading the response.

"No! Target went behind the building. I don't have eyes on him. But he's close to you, Vali. Vero, Lisifrey, go check on Dre," Julian commands. He was our number two. Since Dre is down, hopefully not dead, Julian is now in charge.

"I can get to Dre. He's only about thirty feet from me," I say.

"No! Find our target, González. NOW!"

I don't want to leave Dre splayed out on the ground. I want to help him. I want to keep him alive.

Pop! Pop! Pop!

I push my back against the wall.

Where the hell is that coming from?

There's chaos over the walkies. Lisifrey is screaming. Alan keeps yelling Vero's name over and over. I don't know what I'm supposed to be doing. I can't see what's happening because they are on the other side of the building. There is a flood of gunfire all around me.

"Julian. Can you hear me? Do you know where the incoming gunfire is coming from?"

Our walkies are a mixture of static, screams, and Julian trying to get us information. I can't rely on my team at this moment. All I have is me. I close my eyes and listen. I hear the gunfire coming from Julian's position. That is us shooting. I listen harder. I hear gunfire from what sounds like behind the building we need to get inside of. Our team wouldn't be back there. I snap my eyes open and rush to where I think the gunman is.

I'm right. There he is. His back is to me. He's about six feet tall. There is no way I can take him by myself. I can't kill him from behind because what if it's Belton? He is unloading his gun on someone—maybe it's Vero, maybe he's killing Alan right now. I don't have much time.

I run toward him. I am silent as I rush him. I can't kill him, but I will hurt him. I aim my gun and—

Pop!

My bullet hits his thigh. Blood gushes out of him. He screams in agony. He falls on his back as he grabs his leg. In a matter of seconds, I'm standing above him. I slam my gun into his face shield over and over. The face shield cracks open. I keep on bashing his face. Hatred surges up my body. I see only black. I can't stop. I don't want to stop. I thwack him over and over. It feels good to finally take down a DF officer. It's what I've wanted since they took Mami.

Mami. I see her seeing me in this moment. What would she think? I hear her words: *Protect all creatures large and small. All creatures . . .*

Suddenly I see beyond the black. I see this officer's face below me. Blood is gushing from his nose. His lips are split open. His blue eyes are looking at me, and for a second I feel a tinge of guilt. I did this to him. But then I realize he can easily overpower me. I flip my gun around and press it into his chest. He freezes.

He looks just like the pictures I've memorized of him, only more grotesque. "I've secured the target," I say into the walkie. But no one responds on the other end. The silence grips my heart and threatens to break me, but I don't let this officer know anything is wrong.

"Get up, Belton."

In that instant, he knows we came here for him.

"What do you want?"

Without a word, I shoot him again. This time in his arm. I need him to believe I will kill him, even though I know I can't—at least not until I get the files.

LILIANA

CRRRRRRAAAAACKKKKK!

The sky shatters open. The sound is so loud and piercing, I feel like it's slicing me in two. Everything is shaking and shimmering in my head, my heart, my gut. I cannot tell if my eyes are open or shut. The world is a thick wall of gray smoke. I hear the shrieking of children. I smell the angry stench of fire licking cloth, hair, flesh. I taste bits of rock and sand in my mouth and try to spit them out, but I can't seem to make my mouth work properly. I look around and see the outhouse where Nelini left me her note. Its roof is gone. The tent in front of it, the one I slept in for all these months, is blowing in the wind. The cages inside are exposed like rotting bones.

Is this the end? *I wonder.*

Mi virgencita milagrosa, te doy infinitas gracias por cuidar a mis hijos.

Te pido, por favor acompáñalos, protégelos, libéralos de todo mal y peligro.

I feel the vibrations of my own voice, which means I must still be alive. Still in this body. Which means . . . Rania is gone.

Her burlap sack filled with aqualinium must have exploded into a million fiery bombs. Her selflessness was too much for this world. Her love beyond what this plane was able to nurture. I was supposed to be the one in the flames, but she ended up burning down this hellscape.

The thought of her gone makes me want to collapse. My knees buckle under the weight of my guilt. How could I have let her die? I am ashamed to be alive. Humiliation pulses through me knowing she will never again smell the sweetness of a rose or hear the tenderness of a purring cat. I am too heartbroken to move, too stunned to cry. I just sit here, trying to feel the echo of her hair when I used to braid it. Trying to hold on to her last words. Trying to make this all make sense.

I cannot see much besides the dark smoke, but I pat the ground with my hand to remind me where I am exactly. I pick up a handful of dirt and small pebbles. I let them slip through my fingers. Small pebbles . . . Yes, yes, now I remember. I ran to try and stop Rania from entering the mine. But it was too late. I saw her in the cage going down into the heart of the mine, her dress filled with aqualinium in its hem. I crumpled to the ground and pawed at the dirt around me. I didn't know what else to do. I wanted to be inside the mine where Rania was. My life was supposed to end in there. She was a child and had so much living left to do.

I don't know how long I was on the ground for, but eventually the DF came for me. I tried to fight them off. I thought maybe they would punish me and force me to work inside the mine that night too. But instead, my punishment was to cook dinner for the officers. Unbeknownst to them, I was cooking what I hoped would be their last meal. I spent the rest of the night trying to figure out how to get to Rania. I only had until her shift was over to get the dress off her. But it was impossible to get into the mine without revealing our plan. Rania knew I would never do that. She made me an accomplice in her death.

What kind of world have we created where children feel they must sacrifice themselves for the freedom of others? Are we broken beyond repair? The magnitude of this injustice is too great. I want to give up. But for Rania; for you, Vali; for Ernie; for Isa; and for all the other children, I will not.

As the moon traveled across the night sky, I was forced to accept her choice. I would never see her again. I had failed her, but I couldn't fail everyone else. I told every person in my cage something would be happening soon. I passed messages to the other cages and told them to prepare for freedom. As we prepared for bed, I told moms and dads to stay away from the mine, to make sure to get to the morning roll call late. I told the children to take their time when they woke up; they must slow everything down. I told Isa to run away from the fires, as far away from them as she could.

Pop! Pop! Pop!

Gunfire surrounds me. A searing pain courses up my right hand. It's crushed like a broken wing; blood pours out of what appears to be a gunshot wound. My hand is turned the wrong way, and my wrist dangles like a limp rag. I know this is my hand and I know that I am hurt, but I'm somehow disconnected from this moment. My brain tells me this is my body, but my body seems far away from me.

More gunfire sprays all around me.

My mind tells me I can't sit here any longer and try to figure this all out. I have to get up and get out of here for you and for Ernesto's sake. I push my body up with whatever strength I have left.

And then I run.

I run and run. Remember, mi'ja, I used to say: when they are coming for you, run. You cannot look back. Only forward. Honestly, I do not know which direction I am running in for sure. I just keep running, lurching, searching for any bit of ground to come into view. I swat at my face, trying to wipe my eyes clear, to pull my brain into focus. Slowly, I start to see other bodies take shape in front of me. They are climbing out of the smoke and running too. Pulling each other up and stumbling in different directions. There is so much chaos. I'm searching for SOLIS. I don't see soldiers coming to save us! I see people with broken bones, trying to get away from a fire that reaches to the stars. Am I to blame for this? Did I hurt, maim, and kill these people? *This plan seems so stupid and naive now. How could I have believed some made-up group would risk everything to save us? I wanted to believe there was freedom on the other side of this nightmare. I needed to believe that people cared about us. But now what? Did Rania die for nothing?*

I stop running and look around in horror.

What have I done?

My ears ring. There are sirens wailing now too and another explosion, this one rumbling behind me like slow-moving thunder. The flames look like a kaleidoscope of reds and oranges, churning and charring everything in sight. I turn to see the wall that has kept us trapped in this barbaric nightmare begin to crumble. Part of it falls like a tidal wave, electrical sparks blasting like fireworks.

"Come on!" I shout to everyone and anyone. "RUN! RUN TO THE WALL! ISA, RUN! ESTEBAN, RUN! IF YOU CAN HEAR ME, GOOO!"

The air is getting hotter and thicker, voices and bodies

falling over each other. I feel someone's trembling hand on my leg and stop myself before I trip over the rest of her.

"Get up!" I shout. I have no idea if this person is in one piece, but I grab her hand and pull her up as hard as I can. And we run. More sirens rise up out of the mist, and then another piercing crack from the sky sends us both flying. The ground is coming toward me, and I don't want to take this woman down with me, but I also don't want to let go of her hand. I feel her body crash into me. I scream in pain as my broken hand twists in unnatural directions and blood pours out from the bullet hole.

"I can't do this . . ." she moans.

"You have to!" I bellow. Rania is dead because of me, but this woman will not die too! I pull at whatever limb I can find, and the two of us grope our way to standing, then to running. We keep reaching our arms out, grabbing on to whoever and whatever we can find.

"Keep running! Keep running!" I shriek as she continues on without me. I have to help more people. I can't live with all this death.

I shout at one body that won't move. I shout louder and louder, but I know from the cool of her skin that she is gone, and I want so much to give her freedom.

I plead to the God I have forsaken so many times now to please take her gently, to let her loved ones know she died bravely trying to get her freedom.

And then I keep running.

JESS

CRRRRRRAAAAACKKKKK!

The world is erupting. I thought I was still in the tent, but now there is no difference between inside or outside, up or down. Everyone is staggering and crashing into each other. I try to move forward, but everything turns black. All the air in my lungs rushes out as I open my mouth to scream.

When I come to, every bone in my body feels broken. The dirt beneath me is so hot, I think it may be melting. Or else I am. I squeeze my eyes shut and try to tunnel inward.

"Lili! Lili!"

I know that voice. That's Isa's voice. Shit. Where is Isa? I promised Rania I would take care of that little girl. I had one job to do and now I'm failing that? No!

I spit the dirt and blood out of my mouth and force myself to sit up.

"Isa?" I fumble through the smoke on my knees. "Isa! Isa! It's me! Follow my voice!"

"Lili?!"

"Isa! Follow my voice! I will help you find Liliana!"

I feel like I'm just inches away from her cries, but I cannot find her. I scramble and crawl, shouting her name into the dark, but I am completely lost.

Then I hear a high-pitched whistling noise arcing overhead, and another explosion rocks everything sideways. A huge funnel of smoke rises from the mining pit and bursts into a fiery umbrella of flames overhead.

"Isaaa!"

In the shimmering light, I can see so many people searching, grasping. We are all trying to figure out what is going on, who we can hold on to, and where we can go next.

"Isaaa!" I need to keep this child safe.

"Up ahead!" someone yells. "They blasted open the wall!"

People are clamoring and tripping over each other. I keep calling Isa's name as I pull others to their feet. Some of us are shrieking. Others are stunned into silence. We link arms together, making a human chain. There is a young boy whose hair is on fire, and I join a woman who is dousing the flames with dirt. Another child is shouting prayers into the burning sky. I put her on my back, and we stumble on together until she shouts, "I see her! I see her!" and leaps off, running into someone else's arms.

"Lili?"

"Isa!"

When I find her, I start crying with relief—and awe. Her

little figure etched into the fiery landscape is small but mighty. I pull her into my arms and tell her she is the bravest girl ever. Together, we watch the New American Republic flag burning. It flaps wildly as if it's trying to escape the flames, but it can't.

"Let's go!" I tell Isa. "Let's go find Liliana and get out of here!"

I don't know if that's possible, but I will do whatever it takes to find out. The air is so hot and chaotic with people screaming. I'm trying to follow the crowds, to get Isa toward what looks like an opening in the smoke up ahead.

"Lili!" we call out together.

We pick our way through the rubble and yell her name over and over again. I hold Isa tighter and tighter in my arms. I will not let her be alone. Soon there are throngs of us surging forward, searching for Liliana and anyone else we can find. When we get through the blasted wall of the camp, I almost don't even notice because I'm only looking for Liliana. There are clumps of people huddled together, weeping and coughing. Some are still running in disbelief. Some are being herded onto trucks.

"This way," a calm voice tells me. "It's okay. We're taking you to California."

"What?"

"California!" Isa yells. "Yes, please! Lili told me about this place!"

"I promise," the voice tells me. She shines a flashlight briefly on herself so I can see her open, unmasked face. She has charcoal eyes, thin lips, and a slight accent, but I can't quite place it. She is not wearing a biohazard suit or anything resembling a DF uniform. She's in old-fashioned army fatigues and she tells me she is from a resistance group called SOLIS. She is taking us to sanctuary.

"Sanctuary!"

"Sanctuary!"

People are running, limping, begging to move past me onto the truck now. I want to trust this woman, this promise of hope for Isa, but how do I know?

"Please," Isa tells me. "I want to go eat the mangoes. Come on!"

I want to give her that, I really do. I want to give that to everyone here. What about Liliana? What about all the souls who *deserve* a new life? Who need a home where they are safe and unbound?

"Vamos," a woman behind me says.

I don't know if I'm doing the right thing. I don't know what the right thing is anymore. But I tell Isa to get on the truck while I go look for Liliana. While I make my way back into the desert, from where I came. I don't know if I can find Liliana, but I have to try.

"Please take care of this girl. Her name is Isa," I tell the woman ushering people onto the truck.

Isa looks up at the woman and announces proudly, "I am Isabel Zambrano . . . I am a good child. I obey the rules. I am everything. Blessings to all!"

She blows me a kiss as I continue on searching.

VALI

I push Belton with the butt of my gun, forcing him to walk. He trips and crashes onto the ground. His face is a bloody mess; his thigh and his arm still gush blood. His hands are in handcuffs in front of him. He's in such bad shape, I feel confident I can keep him under control even though he's twice my size.

"Can I have some water?" His voice is barely above a whisper.

"Shut up and walk."

He slowly gets up. We make our way to the building. The reason we are here, the reason behind this nightmare surrounding us.

I feel as if the wind has been knocked out of me as I see Dre's body lying at the entrance of the small brick building. I can't let Belton know my body is screaming to run away, my mind is racing trying to figure out what happened to Vero,

Alan, and Lisifrey. Why the hell can't I get in touch with Julian? Why am I the only one left to finish our mission?

Scattered around Dre are the bodies of three DF officers. In death their blood is indistinguishable from each other. Why is it that in death we are finally equal?

I bend down and take Dre's knife. I make sure Belton sees me put it in my waistband.

I push Belton to the entrance of the building.

"Scan your wrist," I command.

He doesn't move.

"Do it now!"

Nothing.

Without thinking about it, I grab the knife and dig it into the wound on his leg. He screams in pain as he collapses to the ground. There is so much chaos all around us, no one hears him.

"Scan it!" I scream, and I dig deeper into his leg. The knife is almost halfway into his leg.

"OKAY! OKAY! STOP! PLEASE!" he begs.

I grab his wrist and push it toward the scanner. He doesn't resist. An infrared light moves slowly down his wrist. I hold it firmly in place with one hand while the other holds the knife in Belton's leg. The door clicks open, and I throw him into the building.

As soon as we enter, fluorescent lights burst on. It's a very small room, about the size of my bedroom back home in

California. In the center of the room is a computer resting on a metal desk with a chair pushed in. I move Belton to the chair and force him to sit down. I pull out another pair of handcuffs and lock him to the chair. Belton's eyes need to be scanned so we can access the computer. I grab his neck and push his face toward the screen. The computer automatically powers on, ready to scan his eyes, but he keeps his eyes closed.

"Open your eyes!" I say to him.

He ignores me. An error message on the computer screen pops up.

NOT ABLE TO DETECT YOUR RETINA. PLEASE TRY AGAIN.

I know we only have three tries before the computer locks itself down. I spin the chair around and smash my gun into his stomach. He doubles over in pain. I pull his hair and snap his head back hard.

"Open your eyes."

"Go to hell," he says.

"Okay. Have it your way. But I warned you."

I have a small pouch attached to the inside of my ankle. I open it and pull out a needle. I stab it into his neck and shoot in the fluid. Within seconds, he is unconscious. He slouches down the chair. His chin rests against his chest. I grab two metal circular contraptions the size of quarters out of the pouch. I pull his head back and place the two gadgets on his eyes. I swipe my hands over them, and they push open his eyelids. His eyelids want to close, but the metal keeps them open and causes them to bleed. Belton looks *repulsive*. His face is beaten to a bloody pulp, he's been shot multiple times, and his eyes don't look human. I am the person who did this to him. I'm disgusted with myself, but it's too late for self-punishment. I grab him by the hair and push his face toward the computer. The computer rumbles on and scans his eyes.

"Bingo."

I push him away and get to work. I do as I was instructed and place the thumb drive that SOLIS gave me on the center of the screen. It latches onto the screen. It simultaneously downloads everything and releases the virus that will bring the Other 49 to its knees. I begin to rig the room with explosives. In each corner, I place a bomb the size of my finger. I put one on the computer as well. I have one left. It's meant for Belton. I'm supposed to place it on his lap. The last part of my mission is to set off all the bombs. I stare at him. He seems so weak and pathetic, handcuffed to a chair, with his eyes, arms, and legs bleeding. A seventeen-year-old girl took him out. He's the opposite of scary right now, and yet I know while he seems weak at this moment, he is a monster. What do I do with this monstrosity?

I grab the thumb drive and put it in my pouch. I walk to the door, ready to leave him behind, but I hear Mami's words again.

Protect all creatures large and small.

"Damn it!"

I grab the chair and roll it to the door. I uncuff him and

throw him off the chair. His body lands just outside the door. He's lying on top of the dead DF officers. I step over him, and the door slams shut behind me. That's it, I can't go back now. I've disobeyed orders. I'm fucked.

I see him regaining consciousness. I force him to stand up. He can barely walk, but he manages. He's mumbling something that I can't understand. I just keep pushing him forward. I don't know where I am taking him. I'm so mad at myself. But somehow I'm also relieved to have made a decision that Mami would agree with. I need to get him far enough from the building so the explosion won't hurt him. I'll climb back over the wall and leave him to figure out what to do once I'm gone. He won't be my problem. He's so out of it. He keeps stumbling over himself.

"WALK! Stop falling!" I shout at him.

When we get to the wall that surrounds the camp, I hear the unmistakable hum of electricity running through it.

Fuck! is all I can manage to think. I am totally screwed.

What am I supposed to do now? How could they not have kept the wall turned off until I got out? I can't climb over it now. My mind races to find a possible solution. Maybe I should take him toward the explosion. Maybe the wall isn't electrified on the other side of the camp. SOLIS was supposed to breach the camp. I can take him there and turn him in as a prisoner of war. This plan sucks, but it's definitely better than killing him.

Stupid Belton falls again! I am so frustrated, I kick him hard in the stomach. I bend down to pull him to his feet. In my anger, I don't see his head coming toward my face. All of a sudden he headbutts me right in the nose. Blood gushes everywhere as I fall backward. I hit the ground hard. Before I know it, Belton is on top of me, his cuffed hands wrapped around my throat. The pressure on my neck is like nothing I have felt before. I try to breathe, but the air is trapped just outside my lungs. I panic. I kick my legs, trying to squirm out from under him. I start to see specks of black all around me. He's screaming words that I can't make out. This can't be how it ends. I'm so close to Mami. I can't die here.

The black spots have turned into large black circles. I struggle to lift my arm. I have just enough strength to push my finger into his gunshot wound. He screams in pain and loosens his grip around my neck. I dig deeper into him and turn my finger as if it is a key granting me my freedom. He screams even louder. I'm finally able to breathe some air into my lungs. I keep twisting and turning into his wound. He withers in pain, but he won't let go of me. I have no other choice.

Mami, forgive me.

With my free hand, I grab Dre's knife from my waistband and push it into Belton's rib cage. His eyes are stricken with panic. I am instantly ashamed. I have now become the monster. He stumbles back, losing control of his body. He can't stop his backward motion. I know what's going to happen before he does. I can't watch this man die. I shut my eyes. I hear the zapping of electrical currents as he falls onto the wall. I turn away from him. I cannot see another dead body.

This was not how I imagined this mission. I thought we would be heroes. Fighting the bad guys and ensuring our country's future. Instead, I have become a monster just like them. We are all now living in the time of monsters. How do I escape?

I have to leave this godforsaken camp. There is only one way out. I run toward the fire. I run toward the screams and the gunshots. I run toward my people.

The fire reaches the stars. The heat is so intense, the tents have melted into pools of plastic. People as thin as matchsticks run, walk, and limp toward a blown-up section of the wall. Each face is a different combination of blood, sweat, and tears. Some eyes are searching, desperate. Everyone looks so vulnerable, stripped bare. They carry one another, tears streaming down their faces, some fighting to run back and look for a loved one, others crying with joy, freedom almost theirs. Everyone is in a storm of bullets. DF officers shoot at anything that moves. SOLIS soldiers try to protect people as they run out of the camp, but so many are lying on the ground, dead. I want to help, but how can I possibly carry them all in my arms?

LILIANA

And then, through the thick gray smoke, I see the silhouette of someone running toward the hole in the wall. But their body moves differently than ours. They do not appear like the breathing dead. Their body seems strong and agile. They lack our oppressive fear. They are not in our burlap sacks nor do they wear the gas masks and gray bodysuits the DF are so fond of. This person seems to be in army fatigues. Just like the old armies used to wear before California seceded. My mind scrambles in confusion and desperate hope.

Could this be a member of SOLIS?

It must be, right?

Call it faith. Call it chance. Call it a wish and a prayer taking flight, a miracle rising from the ashes of destruction.

All I know is, a flash of light from the burning wall reveals the silhouette's face, and I see that it is really, truly, my daughter. My Valentina!

VALI

I hear, "Valentina!"

I turn toward the voice.

Everything inside me starts trembling. My teeth are chattering; my skin is shuddering. Coming toward me is my mami! This living body, just five feet one inch, but full of all our memories, the heart and brain and blood that gave me life and kept me alive for every second of my seventeen years on Earth.

I dive into her arms and bury my face in her neck. It is so miraculous. I feel her pulse underneath her warm skin; I see her veins crisscrossing in the most spectacular lace of life. I've been running, scavenging, fighting for this moment for so long. For this soft, sacred space between her ear and her chin. This *home*.

"Mami?!" Her hair is singed and clumped with blood. "Are you bleeding? Are you hurt?"

Mami cannot answer me, though. She is sobbing too hard.

Instead, she pulls away from me just enough to inspect me. She runs one of her hands over my face, my shoulders, my arms, gazing at me like I'm some exotic piece of art or maybe a holy figurine. Then she draws me back in again so tight we both gasp, and I hear that familiar smack of her lips as she kisses just below my ear. She kisses me again and again. Those kisses that I was sure I'd never feel again—they propel me through time and space. All those kisses I'd never treasured before—when I woke up or stood before her altar, when she sent me off to school or turned out the light before bed. All the kisses I couldn't even let myself remember until this moment, with her lips tickling my skin.

"Mami, I didn't know what to do," I weep, clutching her tighter and tighter. "I didn't want to leave you, but I thought you said to go! We ran, just like you told us to. Ernie is safe with Tía Luna!"

Mami laughs. And when she does, I see that little scar she has that zigzags across her cheek from an old farming accident. We are here together, alive, and it is all so very real. Mami is staring at me in glassy-eyed disbelief, smoothing my hair back over and over again, saying, "Gracias, Diosito, por protegerlos. Gracias. ¡Gracias!"

LILIANA

There she is in front of me, glorious and brave. Safe and alive.

"¡Gracias!" I repeat over and over. I cannot say it enough.

"¡Gracias!" I touch her face to assure me this is not a dream. She has gotten older, but my baby is still here. I take her in. I hug her.

"¡Gracias!" I look at her again. Her big brown eyes, her crooked smile, her beautifully long eyelashes bring me back to my breath.

"¡Gracias! ¡Gracias!"

She ran through fire, smoke, bullets, and an entire country hell-bent on killing her to get back into my arms. She wraps herself around me. "We have to get out of here, Mami," she says through tears. "SOLIS is here, but it's too dangerous for you to stay."

SOLIS is here.

Nelini, we did it!

Rania, we did it!

Kenna, we did it!

I pull Valentina into my arms and start lurching forward just as the earth starts rumbling again.

And we keep running. I don't know how, but we do. I can't let my Valentina, who I taught to walk and who taught me to mother, be annihilated. I don't know how either of us will survive, but I can't let that stop me.

VALI

No one is going to hurt Mami again. Ever. We are getting out of here alive. I believe in everything now. I believe in my power to get her to safety. I believe in miracles and wild hope. I believe in the unbelievable and the washing away of everything before this moment.

"GO!" I roar.

Mami and I charge forward. We pull people up with us as we run, herding them forcefully. This is our only chance. We have to get to that section of the wall that's been destroyed. It may not be big, but it contains everything.

It is an opening to our new beginning.

As we make our way over the toppled wall, I see the trucks from SOLIS already circled around and gathering everyone they can hold. There are bullets whizzing by and DF officers still staggering out from the camp behind us, so there is no time to pause or look back.

I carry Mami onto the truck. Or is she carrying me?

I don't know anymore who is holding the other up, and it doesn't matter.

We are together. In shock and disbelief but also completely alive.

"Liliana! Liliana!"

Many people on this truck know her and obviously love her.

"My daughter!" she cries. "This is my Valentina!"

The sobs are so loud, they almost drown out the chaos outside. But we can see that the gunshots and explosions are continuing. We have to get out of here before it's too late.

"We are going to drive straight through, and it may get rough. Hold on!" instructs the driver.

As the back of the truck comes down and the engine revs, I hear myself laughing. *Hold on?* How could I ever let go? I will never take this or any moment with Mami for granted again. I will hold on so tight, our flesh will become one.

"But, mi'ja," Mami purrs, wiping at the blood still on my face, "how did you get in? How did you know?"

"Mami, it's so hard to explain."

It's been almost a year since I last saw her. But it's also been a thousand lifetimes. How many people have I seen taken? How many miles have I run? More importantly, how much has Mami had to endure? I want to ask her a million questions. I want to go back in time to when she ran her hands through my hair and lit the candles on her altar next to her portrait of La Virgen. But we cannot go back. We can barely make sense of who, how, or where we are right now. We are all moaning, crying, laughing, the sound of shrapnel pelting our truck in quick succession. The truck is hurtling forward so fast that everyone inside skids and tumbles into each other.

Then I feel something fall from my waistband.

I gasp, realizing what it is.

"Mi'ja, ¿estás bien?" Mami asks.

It's the pouch with the thumb drive.

My mission. Our future.

This thumb drive is meant to save us from the Other 49. It is supposed to allow us to create rain, to control the weather patterns, to end the drought in California, to have hope again.

But at what cost? Who will be made to pay?

Prisoners of war will become slaves, and I can no longer ignore that those who would be enslaved are mothers, daughters, sons, and grandparents. Even though I hate what they did to me, to us, to my mami, I cannot hate them enough to condemn them to servitude.

I pick up the thumb drive. I clasp it in my left hand, squeezing it into a cramped fist. I want to crush it. I want to smash it to smithereens. I want to forget about aqualinium, labors camps, my mission, and SOLIS.

I look to Mami. My right hand is intertwined with hers. Our palms are scratched and scorched and pulsing with life—connected. I want to hold her the whole way back to California. I want to dance with her in Tía Luna's kitchen and have Ernie kick the soccer ball between our legs and for us to all be alive together. I want to be a teenager who worries about teenager things, like homework and pimples, and at the same time I know that I can never go back to that kind of life.

The world is so different now.

I am so different now.

I've watched so many people die, and that includes my former self.

"Mi'ja," Mami whispers. "Look . . ."

I raise my head and look around us in the dark truck, speeding toward whatever comes next. I see pale blue lights rising slowly. A constellation of pinpricks glowing in the night. At first I'm confused. Has the roof opened up to reveal the stars? But then I realize the lights are coming from all the people we are standing with here. The lights shine from their wrists as a message, a demand.

Everyone who is able to raise their hands splays their fingers to form the letter *L*.

"Libertad," Mami says.

"Liberty," I echo.

As the truck rumbles on and I hold Mami and the thumb drive tight, I know these lights, these people, are our only way toward the future.

Mami and I raise our hands together. Even though I don't have a chip anymore, I imagine adding to the blue glow. I see myself as part of this illuminated path forward.

I understand now. I cannot eliminate aqualinium from the Earth, only the systems that enslave the people mining it.

It starts here, in this truck, as we ride into a new dawn.
Freedom is for all of us.
The ones they tried to capture.
The ones they wanted gone.
The ones who will carry on.

AUTHORS' NOTES

The world today is filled with so much pain and injustice. I am often overwhelmed, sometimes to the point of paralysis. On those dark days, I pull out my computer and I write. I create. I imagine. I believe it is the most important thing I can do.

For the past three years, Abby and I wrote *SOLIS*. *SOLIS* is a world created from the bleakest corners of our imaginations. It is scary and violent. It is dark and unjust. But even in the darkest of places there is always light.

Vali, Rania, Liliana, and even Jess have been my light. These beautiful characters have reminded me that kindness can be revolutionary, that bravery can be quiet, that community will save our lives, and that freedom must be fought for.

My dearest reader, *SOLIS* is a clarion call for *you* to fight for freedom. As I write this, in the United States democracy is on the verge of crumbling. The world is being engulfed with the fires of war. Our planet is dying faster than we imagined. And our so-called leaders seem to be chasing their own tails.

This leaves *you* to lead us back to the light. But do not be overwhelmed. You are not alone. Go find the other freedom fighters, the brave ones, the compassionate ones, the ones that can imagine a better world and are inspiring others to go build it with them.

Look to history for guidance. The children of Soweto stood up to the evils of apartheid, young Jewish women in Poland resisted the Nazis and saved countless lives, the mothers of La Plaza de Mayo helped take down the dictatorship in Argentina, and here in the US, queer people refused to die in silence and demanded the nation "ACT UP! Fight back! Fight AIDS!" The injustice these individuals faced seemed insurmountable at the time. The systems of power appeared unbreakable, deeply entrenched in society, their continuation inevitable. And yet the systems fell to the power of the people.

You hold this power. I have faith you will find it inside of you and make this world whole.

—PAOLA MENDOZA

When I was little and scared of the dark, my mom used to tell me that somewhere, right now, the sun is coming up; a new day is beginning.

I try to remind myself of this, especially when life feels like a looming, lonely night. And I'll be honest: It's felt like that a lot over the past few years while we wrote this book. There's been so much hurt, fear, and violence in the world—more than I ever imagined. The social divides and climate catastrophes have reached epic proportions; there are staggering numbers of lives lost or endangered, and somehow we made it through a global pandemic and found new ways to threaten each other and our planet. Many times, I closed my writing notebook and cried because I couldn't figure out which was scarier, the world around me or the one we'd made up on the page.

The world of *SOLIS* is fiction. It's born out of our very real fears about what could happen to this planet and all the people living in it. But I don't think violence is ever the solution, and I don't want young adults to feel like they are solely responsible for saving the Earth or humanity.

I hope you see that *SOLIS* is also a book about resilience and all that we are capable of doing for ourselves and each other. It is inspired by brave revolutionaries. It is a love letter to the ingenious leaders of resistance movements all over the globe and throughout time.

The human spirit continually amazes me. No matter what tragedy unfolds, there are always people picking up the pieces, developing new ways to help, to heal, to regenerate. And no one person can save the world. We told this story from four different points of view because our survival depends on each other. We may each experience this moment differently, but we're all interconnected. It's up to each one of us to choose how we see the world and what we think is possible. We are the only species that has moral sensibilities, cultural evolution, and inventions like artificial intelligence and cheese in a can. We are wise, stupid, brave, terrified, compassionate, egotistical, and daring all in the same breath.

So how do we move forward? How do we care for each other and this planet?

Please, let's not let it get as horrible as it does in the Other 49.

Please, let's lead with love. Let's look each other in the eye and offer compassion, because we are all worthy, we are all human, we are all breathing this same sacred air. Sometimes listening or offering a smile can be revolutionary.

Lastly, we named our resistance movement SOLIS because it is a Spanish name that comes from the Latin *sol*, meaning "sun."

I hope you find sunlight shining through in these pages.

I hope you share it with people and talk about how we can each be a light for one another too.

And I hope if you're afraid of the dark, you know in your heart that somewhere, right now, a new day is beginning.

—ABBY SHER

ACKNOWLEDGMENTS

Michael, through pandemics, life transitions, and adventures around the world, you have been my constant. Your unwavering faith in me for over twenty years allowed me to become the artist I am today. One family forever!

Mateo, your imagination inspires me always. Thank you for brainstorming story ideas for this book. You make me better. You made this book better.

Mamá, Rick, Pamela, Victoria, Brandon, Ryan, and the Skolniks, you were with me every step of the way. I am because you are.

Abby, thank you for your collaboration in imagining *SOLIS*. You are a reminder that art will always save us.

Jose, thank you for teaching me the history of the Filipino people's fight for freedom. Nelini, Kenna, Rania, Vali, and Liliana pay homage to their struggle. They serve as a reminder that our stories of liberation are always bound to one another.

Sarah Sophie, Ginny, Meredith, Nelini, Paula, Shruti, and Adrianne, getting into good trouble with you not only makes the world better, it keeps me dancing to the beat of our revolution. You inspire me to never stop fighting. Each of you are in these pages.

Tracey, Rupa, Bridgit, Tanya, and the rest of the Pop Culture Collaborative family, thank you for supporting my work for all these years. You gave me the ability to write *SOLIS*. Together we will rewrite the future!

Bridget and Rania, thank you for picking up the phone and answering all my questions. You didn't have to trust a stranger, but I am so grateful you did.

Yara, Esther, Eisa, Sarah, SSF, and Becky: my hermanas, my biggest cheerleaders, the ones who got me through the pandemic and a divorce, your friendship is my balm, your laughter my joy, your love my foundation.

Chase, you were not afraid of my scars. You expanded my world. Thank you for being on this journey for forever.

—PAOLA MENDOZA

We are thankful for so many people who made this book possible.

Thank you thank you to my dearest friends and mentors for seeing me through this process: Mary Bergstrom, Deborah Goldstein, Gabriella Di Maggio, Joselin Linder, Jocelyn Jane Cox, Thea Cogan-Drew, Emily Sims, Gabra Zackman, Sara Moss, Samantha Karpel, Joy Smith, Haley Dapkus, Susan

Shapiro, V.C. Chickering, Judy Batalion, Megan Grano, and so many more.

Thank you to Paola, who challenged me to dig deeper and find hope through the fear; to push for art that propels change.

And thank you to my amazing family—Jason, Sonya, Zev, Sam, and Lucy—for holding my hand, forcing me to take dance breaks, and reminding me that love is always healing and usually involves popcorn.

—ABBY SHER

Thank you to our warrior editor Stacey Barney, for believing in us and continually being our champion. Thank you to her incredible team at Penguin Random House—Caitlin Tutterow, Jenny Ly, Sarah Sather, and Nancy Paulsen. Thank you to Mollie Glick and Via Romano at CAA for keeping us focused and motivated. Thank you to Dana Lédl for bringing our characters to life and to Maria Fazio and Kathryn Li for the beautiful book design. Thank you to Linda Yvette Chávez for asking the tough questions and opening up infinite possibilities for answers. Thank you to Asher Goldstein, Ron Najor, and the phenomenal team at Macro Productions—Greta Fuentes, Jelani Johnson, and Natalie Guerrero.

And thank *you*, for reading these words, turning these pages, and sharing our story.

—PAOLA & ABBY

READ AN EXCERPT FROM THE HEART-POUNDING COMPANION TO *SOLIS*

CHAPTER 1

It took fifteen steps for her to die.

Fifteen—one for each year of her life before they snuffed it out.

I was supposed to be doing homework. I actually *was* doing homework, but my phone kept buzzing, so I tapped on the notifications, and there she was.

I never did learn her name. In the reports they would call her "an illegal fifteen-year-old" or "a fifteen-year-old immigrant." It depended on who was talking.

The underground reporters would also call her *brave, defiant, fearless*.

And the government news would call her *disease-ridden, illegal, criminal*.

✖

BUT AS I watched it with my own eyes, I saw that she was just a girl my age. Wearing a faded Mickey Mouse T-shirt and jean shorts that were rolled over on top but still looked like they might fall off her skinny waist. She had somehow gotten over a line of concrete ballasts and the chain-link fence stretching across the burnt-out field between Tijuana and San Diego. That rusty, mangled barricade that was supposed to keep people on the Tijuana side. It stood there as a scar. A reminder. A warning. Its sole purpose was to say

STAY OUT. YOU DON'T BELONG HERE.

That girl in the Mickey Mouse shirt had no time for warnings. She had no interest in being intimidated. She looked completely unafraid as she stepped away from the fence, entering the no-man's-land between Mexico and the United States. The girl was alone, unarmed. Her dark hair was tied back in a bouncy ponytail, and she had a bright red scratch under her left eye. Besides that, her face looked clear, even calm, as she made her way across the dusty strip of scrubland between Tijuana and the wall.

Or really, the Wall. The Great American Wall.

There was nothing great about it. More like grotesque. It blocked out the sky, with fifty-foot-tall reinforced steel slats and thick metal mesh in between. Every few feet there were coils of barbed wire strung across, and on top there was a maze of cables spitting out electricity. The government had spent gazillions of dollars and called in all the Reserves to help build this monstrosity. Sealing us off from the rest of the Americas.

Stop where you are! snarled a voice through a speaker by the Wall.

Technically, that girl wasn't even on United States soil. But as the President loved to say, America was the greatest nation in the history of greatness, and we needed to do whatever it took to protect our sacred borders. That was why there was a platoon of Border Patrol officers lined up on top of the Wall. Green zombies, I called them. Standing at attention in their olive-colored uniforms with pale, expressionless faces. They had the newest AK-87s strapped to their backs and German shepherds circling at their feet as they stared down that girl.

Because this was their land.

Because it was their duty to preserve and defend the United States of America.

Because whatever this fifteen-year-old intended, walking across in her flip-flops and saggy shorts, she had now become a national threat.

✖

I WAS SO scared and awestruck by that girl's slow, deliberate steps forward. I could even hear myself panting for her as I watched.

"Mi'ja, what are you doing?" Mami asked me. "If you're done with your homework, get ready for bed."

"Wait. You have to see this."

"No, I don't."

"Yes, Mami, you do," my little brother, Ernie, said, padding in from the bathroom in his pj's. Last I knew, he was watching soccer on his phone, but he must've gotten the same alerts as me. "Something weird is going on at the Wall," he reported.

Mami hated all the notifications and interruptions from our phones, even if we had saved up and paid for them with our own money. But when Ernie came in and made that announcement, Mami stopped wiping the kitchen counter and marched over to stand behind me at the table.

"¿Qué es eso? I can't even see. The screen is too small," she sighed.

Mami loved to tell us how when our family first came to this country, we watched the same show, all together, on a single television. Of course, that was before the government took over the broadcasting system. Before they censored any newscasters who disagreed or said too much, any movies or shows that seemed unpatriotic. If we wanted to see anything honest or original these days, we had to watch someone's livestream on the dark web. Which is what we were doing now. The three of us pressed our heads together, watching the image blink in and out because of the poor connection. The camera panned around, showing faces caught between hope and panic.

"I don't like this," Ernie said. I didn't either, but we couldn't turn away from the screen. We couldn't move. We could only gape at this staticky footage as that gutsy girl planted each foot down—one, two, three.

There were shouts from the crowd of people in Tijuana gathering behind the barricade:

¿Qué estás haciendo? ¡Cuidado!

An airhorn blasted. Another green zombie shouted through the speakers:

Get back behind the fence! he bellowed. *You are not permitted on US soil. We repeat, you are not permitted on US soil!*

The girl paused and raised both of her hands in the air to show that she meant no harm. She squinted into the bright West Coast sun with a sort of half grin. Her arms were loose and gawky. I wondered if she was born with this kind of wild bravery or if she'd just already lost too much to care.

She stepped forward again.

"Why's she doing that?" whispered Ernie. "Why isn't she listening to them?"

I tried to mumble some sort of response, but my tongue felt too big for my mouth. I flipped to another livestream in Tijuana—they were all filming this girl now. Some from so far away, she looked like a speck creeping across the frame, in between the concrete posts. Others zoomed in so close, I swear I could see the hairs in that girl's nose. Yes, we were watching her on a screen from thousands of miles away, in the safety of a dusky Vermont evening. But my whole body was trembling for her. I wished I had even a smidge of her courage.

There is no trespassing in the demilitarized zone! the zombies ordered again. *We repeat, no trespassing in the demilitarized zone!*

"Dios mío," Mami said in a low voice, clicking her tongue. She made the sign of the cross, and I swallowed hard. Mami was as tough as they came, the creases around her eyes holding on to all her worry and pain so that she could always face the world with composure. If she was asking God for help, then this was definitely a moment of truth.

Meanwhile, the girl took another step forward. And another. She looked like she was full-on smiling now. At least, that's how I want to remember her.

This is your last warning! roared the zombies.

¡Eres un héroe! ¡Cuidado! yelled the crowd behind her in Tijuana. I could hear people chanting from behind the Wall in San Diego. It sounded like they were saying, *Let her through! Let her through!*

The voices on all sides swelled and lifted her up so she looked like she was floating those last few steps. Eleven, twelve.

I was counting in my head.

She had just put down her flip-flop for the fifteenth time when the ground exploded underneath her. The sudden flares of orange, yellow, and red slashing through her. Blowing her into bits. Turning her into dust.

Everything shuddered around me. I felt like that bomb had just detonated inside my gut, the shock waves rumbling through me. The fierce blast of flames was the sharpest color

I'd ever known. And scariest of all, there was no sound. Or, really, there was only the *absence* of sound. Like the whole world had just been punctured and we had to suck in whatever air was left in one giant gasp, holding it all in for as long as we could.

Ernie was the first one to lose it. "What happened? Where'd she go? How come we can't see her?" he said, panicking.

"She's . . . she's," I stammered. I didn't know how to explain what had just happened—to him or to myself. "Mami?"

Mami just stood there, watching the screen, as Ernie and I let a thousand unanswerable questions dribble out of our mouths. We needed to fill all the space between us. To keep talking, because talking was breathing, and breathing was living, and living meant we still existed even if it was in some crazy effed-up world where a fifteen-year-old girl was blown up because she tried to cross the border.

"Mami, did you see what happened?" I begged. When I couldn't take Mami's silence anymore, I grabbed her warm wrist and squeezed.

"Sí, claro que sí," Mami murmured. Seeing Mami this disturbed only made it more horrible, more real. She exhaled slowly, the air whistling through her teeth. Then she clenched her eyes shut, like she was trying to erase what she'd just seen on my screen. "It is a land mine, mi'ja. Like in Colombia."

"What?" I shouted. As if my anger could change what had just occurred. Although maybe it did, because the picture of the girl in flames went dark. The connection severed.

I flipped to a different livestream again. The first one I found was from someone standing on the San Diego side of the Wall. I heard people wailing and shouting, *They killed her! They killed her!*

Then I saw a mad rush of bodies, pushing and shoving their way toward the Wall. Hurling themselves at the steel slats, scraping and kicking at the mesh in between.

A stampede of green zombies charged into the fray. It looked like there were just as many of them on the ground in San Diego as there were on top of the Wall. Maybe more. Now they were unleashing their German shepherds on the American side. The canines grunting and snapping.

There was a blast of white.

Whoever was filming our livestream started shaking and running. Shouting, *Cover your mouths! Run!*

It sounded like the Border Patrol officers on the American side were now launching tear gas canisters at the scrambling crowd in San Diego.

"Dios mío," Mami gasped again.

There were bodies writhing and twisting on the ground. They clawed at each other, desperate for pockets of fresh air. Then there was a thud. All we could see on my phone was the dusty ground—a flood of sneakers, flip-flops, and bare feet running by.

"No!" I pleaded. I wanted to reach through the screen and save whoever had just gone down, but I had to find another feed to see what was happening. I scrolled through image after image. The crowds on both sides of the Wall were multiplying by the second now. Surging with rage and heartache. Shouting into their screens or at the Border Patrol helicopters swooping in and circling overhead.

In Tijuana, there were people scaling the chain-link fence. Tripping over themselves as they charged toward the bits of that broken girl.

¡Era una niña! they wailed. Mothers clutched their children, tears coursing down their cheeks.

In San Diego, there were people banging rocks on the Great Grotesque Wall. Pounding and hammering at the ballasts, like a growing thunder.

No more walls! No more deaths! they yelled. There were thousands of hands grabbing, scratching. Trying to rip apart the steel, the barbed wire, the hatred that went into building the Wall. The green helicopters hovered over them like a venomous cloud.

"What are the helicopters for? Are they gonna hurt more people?" Ernie asked in a tiny voice.

"I don't think so. No, they cannot," Mami said, reaching for my phone, maybe to shut it off and protect us from seeing any more. Only, as she did, a new and horrifying sound belted out from my screen.

Tet-tet-tet-tet-tet-tet-tet!

The helicopters were shooting into the crowds on both sides.

"No!" I screamed.

"Dios mío santísimo . . ."

The shrieks and moans were piling on top of each other. It didn't matter what language they spoke; they were all crying *Help!* Ernie buried his head in Mami's chest.

"Wait! What if . . . what if Tía Luna's there?" I sputtered.

Mami lunged at the kitchen counter to get her phone.

"Todo va estar bien. Tranquilos," was all she'd say as she dialed her sister's number.

"Call Tía Luna!" I screamed at my phone. It couldn't recognize my voice when I was this frantic and screechy, though. So I tried to type in her name, my fingers jerking and stuttering from key to key.

A stale recording came on at the other end of the phone:

Your request cannot be processed at this time. Please hang up and try again.

Mami was pacing across the linoleum, hanging up and trying again. Hanging up and trying again.

"Do you think she's there?" I asked. "She wouldn't go there, would she?"

"No. No creo," Mami said, her face a knot of pain and anger. She put down her phone for a brief moment and clasped her hands together in front of our kitchen window like she was begging the sky to tell her something else.

"I don't get it," Ernie whimpered. "What's going on?"

There were so many shots coming from my screen now. I couldn't count them anymore. I couldn't do anything. The gap between us and whatever was going on at the border widening like a giant hole.

Dividing us into here and there.

Before and after.

"We know nothing," Mami told us. "We don't know if Tía Luna is there or if . . ."

And then it was all cut off.

Our phones went dark. There was no sound, no image. No connection to whatever was unraveling on the other side of the country. Just a blank screen. We held our breath and waited, pinched with fear.

And then, a few moments later, a new, haunting image flickered on. I'd never seen anything like this being broadcast before. It was a large desk in the middle of a bare room. There were stark gray cinder-block walls behind it, interrupted only by a portrait of the President and an empty wooden chair.

I flipped to another feed, and another. But they were all showing the same thing. The same desk, the same wall, the same portrait.

As if to wipe away everything that had just happened.

As if to wipe *us* all away.

Photo Credit: Shayan Asgharnia

PAOLA MENDOZA is an author, film director, activist, and artist working at the leading edge of human rights. A cofounder of the Women's March, she served as its artistic director. Her writing has appeared in *The New York Times*, *HuffPost*, *Glamour*, *Elle*, and *InStyle*. Paola is a cofounder of the Resistance Revival Chorus, the Soze Agency, and the Meteor.

Photo Credit: Lee Seidenberg

ABBY SHER is an award-winning writer and performer. She is the author of *Miss You Love You Hate You Bye*; *All the Ways the World Can End*; *Breaking Free*; *Amen, Amen, Amen: Memoir of a Girl Who Couldn't Stop Praying*; and *Kissing Snowflakes*.